"I must say you've been very clever."

Benet's face was as unyielding as marble. "Someone with family connections who already worked for my gallery, a girl who could put on such an act of honesty and integrity she even had me fooled....

What's in it for you, Kirsten? A cut of the profits? Or is your partner such a fantastic lover you were besotted enough to agree to any of his devious schemes?"

"No!" The denial was torn from her in an anguished gasp. "You can't really think that I knew—"

But he did. She stared at him with stricken eyes. He actually believed her a willing accomplice in the plot to defraud him.

Books by Stacy Absalom

HARLEQUIN ROMANCE
2581 – KNAVE OF HEARTS
2671 – THE PASSION AND THE PAIN

These books may be available at your local bookseller.

Don't miss any of our special offers. Write to us at the following address for information on our newest releases.

Harlequin Reader Service
P.O. Box 52040, Phoenix, AZ 85072-2040
Canadian address: P.O. Box 2800, Postal Station A,
5170 Yonge St., Willowdale, Ont. M2N 6J3

The Passion and the Pain

Stacy Absalom

Harlequin Books

TORONTO • NEW YORK • LONDON
AMSTERDAM • PARIS • SYDNEY • HAMBURG
STOCKHOLM • ATHENS • TOKYO • MILAN

Original hardcover edition published in 1984
by Mills & Boon Limited

ISBN 0-373-02671-4

Harlequin Romance first edition February 1985

having to feel beholden to her aunt's influence, she had realised she would be a fool to turn down the job when it was offered to her. Not only would her regular salary help to keep the small antique shop enterprise afloat, she would also be gaining valuable experience at the top end of the antiques market.

And anyway, Aunt Gussie's machinations hadn't got her anywhere, Kirsten thought with a grin. In the six months she had been working as Davina's secretary, she hadn't as much as glimpsed the owner of the gallery. Most of Benet Saker's time was divided between the gallery in Mayfair that was now his headquarters and the one he had recently opened in New York. He left the running of the original gallery started by his father in Davina's capable hands, and on the very rare occasions when his presence was needed in the West Country, Davina took good care to keep him exclusively to herself. Whether this was to prevent the staff going over her head and taking any complaints or requests straight to the top, or whether she had a more personal reason for monopolising his time, Kirsten had no idea.

The fact that her aunt couldn't help coupling her with Benet Saker in her mind was enough to make Kirsten actively want to avoid meeting him, or at the very least, to be grateful that their paths had never crossed. And now Benet Saker was on the other side of that communicating door and at any moment the summons could come for her to go in. Of course, she was curious about him but it wasn't only curiosity that was making her unable to concentrate on her work, it was excitement too.

She had had a hunch as soon as Jude Ofield had shown her that portfolio of century-old drawings that this was an important find and the fact that Benet Saker had come hurrying all the way from London himself to see them bore out that hunch. If they were both right then the proceeds from the sale of the drawings would keep Jude in paint and canvas for years to come, not to mention food and rent. And the commission she would draw herself on the sale would be a useful boost to the business she and Poppy were trying so hard to get off the ground.

Kirsten was grateful to Jude for giving her this wonderful opportunity. There had been nothing to prevent his bringing the valuable drawings along to the Saker Galleries himself and saving the necessity of paying two lots of commission, the gallery's and her own. But when she had pointed this out to him, Jude wouldn't hear of it, insisting that as it had been Kirsten's idea to turn what he called 'a bit of family clutter' into cash—an idea that had apparently never occurred to him even when he didn't know where his next week's rent was coming from—it was only fair that she should benefit from it.

Kirsten shook her head over his unworldliness. It wasn't as if Jude owed her any favours. She wasn't a special friend of his, although he had made several good-natured passes at her. She hadn't even known him all that long. It was barely five weeks, she realised with surprise, doing a rapid calculation in her head, since the burly artist had first stopped by the stall she and Poppy took every Sunday at one of the local antique markets and they had got talking.

There was nothing at all romantic in the friendship that had developed between them, however much Poppy liked to imagine there was. Kirsten liked Jude: he brought out her mothering instincts. For a man built more like a rugby forward than a starving artist he seemed singularly helpless at looking after himself. And though she was sometimes shocked by his more Bohemian attitudes, she understood his resentment towards galleries like Sakers who weren't interested in an artist until he was long dead. But while she defended her business, arguing that surely it was better for the work of artists and craftsmen to change hands at inflated prices rather than be lost forever on some rubbish tip, she had often asked him back to the flat over the shop for supper, and had occasionally been asked back to his studio in return.

It had been on one of these visits that Jude had casually shown her the portfolio of old drawings that had now brought Benet Saker so promptly from London. So casually that it was obvious he had no great feeling for the fact that they were almost a family heirloom, so she had felt little compunction in suggesting he should turn them into cash to make his living conditions a bit easier.

'Sell them?' Kirsten remembered his vague astonishment.

She had glanced at the sliding heap of old newspapers, discarded scraps of his own very modernistic work and accumulated junk he had been rummaging through to retrieve the drawings, and shuddered. 'Haven't you any idea how valuable these could be?'

But he had only shrugged. 'I'm interested in my *own* work, not some long-dead ancestor's.'

'So why not let them go to someone who *would* value them, and use the money to live on while you get on with your own work?' she had pressed, and Jude had grinned that wide, white, ingenuous grin as if she had thought of something clever.

Kirsten glanced impatiently at her watch again. Perhaps she wasn't going to be needed after all. Perhaps Benet Saker would just take the drawings back to London with him without bothering to talk to her. Before she could fully realise how disappointed that thought made her, the intercom buzzed, making her jump.

'Right away, Miss Coyle,' she responded to the crisp instruction to come in. But she paused long enough to check in her compact mirror that her mop of coppery hair was reasonably tidy and that there were no smudges on her face from the typewriter ribbon. Greenish eyes stared back at her with just a tinge of apprehension. Then, snapping the compact shut, she squared her shoulders and tapped on the communicating door.

Her eyes flew at once to the man leaning over the drawings spread out on the top of Davina's desk, handling with extreme care the paper that had yellowed with age at the edges, but he gave her only the most cursory of glances when Davina said, 'This is Kirsten, the girl who brought the drawings in, Benet.'

Kirsten on the other hand couldn't help staring and it wasn't only out of curiosity about the man her aunt so foolishly dreamed of as a husband for her. Benet Saker was quite a legend in their sleepy old town, the local boy who had become something of a tycoon in the antique art world with a formidable reputation for one so young—thirty-four, according to the article Kirsten had seen recently in an art magazine—so she could be forgiven for staring.

And he was something to stare at: tall, broad-shouldered and lean-hipped in impeccable cavalry drills with a roll-neck sweater that looked like cashmere beneath a suede jacket as supple as a second skin. He had a lean, clever face with a square chin and a firm mouth that looked as if he knew what he wanted and always got it, his fair skin an arresting contrast with the jet-black hair that fell just short of his collar. With his winging eyebrows and sweeping dark lashes, his well-manicured hands with their long, slim fingers, he might have looked effeminate, yet somehow he managed to give off powerful waves that were all male. But the most riveting thing about him was his incredibly blue eyes.

Eyes that blue Kirsten had only come across once before—on Jude Ofield—but where on the red-headed, red-bearded Jude they were exceptional only in their innocent guilelessness, on Benet Saker, fringed by those dark lashes, they had an extraordinary impact, so that she hardly heard Davina saying, 'Mr Saker agrees with me that you've made a remarkable find, Kirsten.'

Kirsten was suddenly aware that those eyes were now directed unwaveringly at her, studying her in expressionless silence until she felt like a specimen under a microscope.

'Remarkable indeed,' he said at last, his voice as smooth as silk, but then he went on with a hint of steel, 'Even more remarkable is how a couple of dozen hitherto unknown Winslow Homer drawings come to be in the possession of our little secretary!'

Kirsten gasped. Just what was he trying to accuse her of? Surely he couldn't think . . . her face flaming at the insulting implication, her hands curling into fists, she flung at him, 'I haven't stolen them, if that's what you're hinting!'

The dark eyebrows lifted, giving him the look of a satyr.

'Who said anything about them being stolen?' he said softly.

'You did. At least—' For just a moment she felt uncertain under that penetratingly satirical gaze, then her chin came up defiantly. No one had ever accused her of dishonesty before. Benet Saker might have an exaggerated opinion of his own importance, but she wasn't going to let him browbeat her. 'You made it sound as if that was what you meant.'

He gave a long-suffering sigh. 'How long have you been working at Saker Galleries?'

His question threw her into confusion again. 'S-six months.'

'Long enough, surely, to know how important background information about any work of art is, particularly something as potentially valuable as these?' The well-manicured hands gestured towards the drawings on the desk and his voice held a sting of reproof.

Kirsten did know, of course, and she felt so foolish at

leaping immediately on to the defensive that she blushed fierily.

'So let's begin with ownership,' he suggested coldly. 'The drawings are your property?'

'No, they belong to a friend. And *he* didn't steal them either,' she couldn't resist adding, because for all he was trying to put her in the wrong, he *had* made it sound like an accusation and she resented it.

But as she saw Benet Saker's mouth tighten she regretted that dig. She might be perfectly justified in feeling resentful at his arrogant attitude, but she knew she couldn't let that resentment get in the way of what was, after all, purely a business matter.

'This friend's family came originally from the Tynemouth area where, as I'm sure you know, Winslow Homer spent a year or so in the early eighteen eighties,' she went on to explain in a more conciliatory tone.

Jude had told her the story that had been handed down in his family over several generations, of how the American artist, on a visit to the North of England, had taken lodgings with Jude's ancestor and had enjoyed not only bed and board but also the daughter of the house to share that bed, and on returning to his own country had left behind a token of his regard, the baby who was to become Jude's great-grandfather, along with the portfolio of drawings as a sort of thank-you present. Kirsten repeated a rather less colourful version of this story to Benet Saker.

'Is there any written provenance?' Davina asked eagerly when Kirsten came to the end of her explanation. 'Any old letters or wills mentioning the drawings?'

Kirsten shook her head, regretfully having to admit, 'Apparently not.' She had asked Jude the same question herself, but as he had pointed out, his family had been humble folk and would have been too poor to bother with wills. And as for letters—if there ever had been any—none had survived that he knew of. The wonder was that the drawings themselves had survived intact.

Davina seemed about to press the point, but Benet Saker broke in dismissively, 'Well, we must thank Kirsten for bringing the drawings to our attention.' He took out a leather-bound notebook and unscrewed the cap of a gold pen. 'Now, if you'll let me have this friend's name and address . . .'

Kirsten decided she had been right when she had once told her aunt she would probably hate Benet Saker on sight. She didn't like him at all. He was still every bit as superior and condescending as she remembered him from that one meeting in her childhood. And he obviously didn't think very much of her either, treating her as an unreliable witness whose word was suspect.

She drew herself up stiffly. 'I'm sorry, but I can't do that.'

The blue eyes narrowed and that square chin suddenly looked very formidable. 'Forgive me, but I was under the impression the drawings were being offered for sale,' he said coldly. 'If you've brought me down here on a wild-goose chase . . .'

'Th-they *are* for sale.' The words came out as little more than a hoarse croak because of the stupidly apprehensive fluttering in her throat.

'So how do you expect me to go about selling them if you can't—or won't—put me in touch with the owner? That was a very convincing little story you told us—' the emphasis he put on the word 'story' was quite unmistakable '—but surely even you can see it has to be checked out. Saker Galleries can't risk handling anything that's even remotely suspect.'

Kirsten squirmed under his sarcasm and longed to prick this man's arrogant conceit with the scathing words that were rising to her tongue. But though she had every reason to resent his tone, she knew enough about the workings of the antique art world to know he had some justification for what he was saying. It had seemed a wonderful opportunity when Jude had insisted on her arranging the sale of the drawings for him, but suddenly Kirsten wasn't so sure of the ethics of her position, working on her own behalf while she was still employed at the gallery. But there was no backing out now. 'He—my friend asked me to handle his side of the business,' she blurted out, hoping the tremble in her voice wasn't too apparent.

'You!' Davina Coyle looked as amazed as if the type-writer had jumped up and answered her back.

'He wants *you* to act for him?' Benet Saker looked equally incredulous, his dark brows drawing together in a thunderous frown.

Kirsten quailed but stuck to her guns. 'He—he wishes to remain anonymous.'

'Oh does he! Well, I hope you warned him it could cost him a lot of money, hiding behind your skirts.' Benet Saker closed his notebook with an angry snap. 'Saker Galleries have a reputation to uphold. We certainly can't offer these at auction as authentic if we can't check out their history for ourselves.'

Kirsten had explained this to Jude, but characteristically he had only laughed. 'You know what I think of art dealers, my pet, growing fat on the work of poor devils who mostly died of starvation. The day *I* walk through the door of any gallery will be the day they're showing *my* work, and not before. Any dealer worth his salt can see what those drawings are. So you just keep my name out of it, understand? I've got better things to do with my time than answer their damfool questions.'

'I've checked his claims,' Kirsten said doggedly. 'Last week, when I took two days of my holiday to go up to Tynemouth. And it all ties in, beginning with the registra-tion of his mother's birth; names, dates, births, marriages, in all the right places and at all the right times, going back to the unmarried girl who gave birth to my friend's great-grandfather. I've written it all out—' She picked up the empty folder and took a typed sheet out of the pocket, holding it out to Benet Saker.

'And we're expected to take your word for all this?' Davina was outraged as she glanced at the document in their boss's hand. 'Surely you must have told your friend you're only the secretary here?'

Kirsten flushed at her disparaging tone, but had to admit it must look very odd to them when they didn't know she also ran her own business. She sighed. It had seemed perfectly straightforward when she had agreed to handle the sale of the drawings for Jude. Naïvely, she had supposed handing the portfolio and the family tree she had drawn up over to Davina would be the sum total of her involvement. Certainly she hadn't expected to be treated as a hostile witness in an interrogation like this. For the first time it occurred to her what thin ice she was skating on. Any minute now she could find herself out of a job.

'M-my friend doesn't know me as the secretary here at Saker Galleries,' she confessed. 'At least, he knows I work here, but he knows me best as an antique dealer. I'm in partnership with a friend in a little shop just off Cathedral Close, but of course it doesn't pay enough to support us both yet, so I help out by working here . . .' Her voice died away as she caught sight of Davina's face.

Short and fairly sturdy herself, with a mop of hair that went its own way however hard she tried to control it, Kirsten had always envied Davina's ethereal beauty; slightly taller than average, but very slender with a graceful neck and delicate features framed in gleaming blonde hair caught softly into a chignon at the back of her head, leaving curly tendrils to brush her jawline. But there was nothing ethereal about Davina's expression at that moment.

'You run your own business as well as working for me!' she exploded. 'Of all the deceitful, underhand tricks. I trusted you, Kirsten, and this is how you repay me. All the time you've been using your confidential position here to snoop and spy.'

'That's not true!' Kirsten protested indignantly. 'Oh, I admit that when my aunt used her influence to get me this job I thought it would be good experience, but I haven't betrayed any trust or turned any confidential matters I might have learned here to my own advantage. I've done nothing that could possibly harm the gallery. How could I?'

'I'm rather inclined to agree with her, Davina,' Benet Saker said surprisingly, adding with obvious amusement, 'How could her little junk shop possibly harm us?'

Kirsten supposed she should have been glad he was taking her part, but his patronising tone caught her on the raw and before she could hold her volatile temper she turned on him: 'It's not everyone who has the good fortune to have a thriving antique gallery handed to them on a plate,' she snapped with withering scorn. 'Some of us have to do things the hard way, starting from the bottom with a junk shop, as you so contemptuously put it.'

His eyes widened in surprise at her unexpected attack and though getting under his guard gave her a certain satisfaction, she regretted losing her temper, especially when Davina said tightly, 'That does it! Not only deceitful but insolent, too. Your services are no longer required here, Kirsten, and if your aunt wants to know the reason why, I shall be only too glad to tell her.'

Kirsten's heart lurched then sank right down into her knee-high boots. She had blown it! No financial security from the sale of the drawings for Jude, no commission for herself—and no job. And not only was it back to the breadline, but she was going to have to face Aunt Gussie's monumental wrath when she heard what had happened. And one look at Davina's face told her there was no hope of keeping the reason for her sacking quiet. Mortifyingly aware of Benet Saker's silent witness to her humiliation, she blinked back the tears that were misting her stormy green eyes and began to gather up the scattered drawings.

'You mean they sacked you on the spot!' Jude was working at his easel when Kirsten interrupted him in the evening of the same day. His usually mild blue eyes sparked with indignation and his curly beard actually seemed to bristle.

His studio, at the top of a dilapidated house in a once elegant but now run-down terrace on the far side of the park, was in its usual state of chaos: the big window grimy, the bare floorboards paint-spattered to an uneven carpet of many colours. Unsold canvases were stacked against the walls and every inch of space, including the unmade bed in one corner, was strewn with sketches or painting materials.

'They can't do that.' He flung down his paintbrush on to the littered table that stood beside his easel.

'They haven't *exactly* sacked me . . .' Kirsten began to explain how, just as she was about to slink, chastened, out of Davina's office, Benet Saker had said coolly, 'While I wouldn't dream of interfering with the way you run the gallery here, Davina, I do think Kirsten ought to stay around, at least until we've sorted out the business of these drawings.'

'Hah! They're willing to keep you on just as long as there's something in it for them,' Jude said in disgust. 'I suppose you told them to stuff their job.'

'Well, no . . .' Kirsten wasn't proud of the fact that her first reaction had been of profound relief that Aunt Gussie wouldn't have to hear of her disgrace—yet. She supposed it was rather weak-kneed of her, and it would have served Benet Saker right if she had told him the drawings were no longer on offer.

'Of course, I can take the drawings elsewhere if that's what you want, Jude.' She was, after all, acting on his instructions, but she also felt under an obligation to do what she knew was best for him in spite of her personal feelings. 'But Sakers is the best firm to handle the sale. Winslow Homer was an American artist, as you well know, so it's in the States that there's going to be most interest in his work. And with Sakers having a branch in New York they're in a good position to get the utmost publicity for the sale.'

Given Jude's indignation at the news of her threatened dismissal and his prejudice against art dealers in general, she expected him to put up an argument, but surprisingly he only hugged her, grinning broadly. 'You're the boss, love. The drawings stay with Sakers if you say so.'

He was holding her too closely for her to see his face, but he sounded almost as if he was enjoying some private joke when he added, 'So the great Benet Saker came running all the way from London to take a look at my drawings . . .'

'Yes.' Kirsten eased back from his bear-like hug to look up at him. 'And as he *is* here, won't you change your mind and talk to him, Jude? The fact that there's no written provenance to support the authenticity of the drawings is a drawback, and it could make a big difference to the price they'll fetch at auction if Mr Saker can satisfy himself personally about their history.'

'Oh, don't start on that tack again.' Jude's arms fell away from her and he hunched his big shoulders irritably. 'I told you—I don't want to be bothered.'

'But wouldn't it be worth the bother if you can be sure of getting the top price?' she persisted. 'It would mean you could afford somewhere decent to live, for one thing.' She cast a quick glance of distaste at the cluttered and frankly rather squalid studio. 'You can't *like* having to work and sleep in the same room.'

'It suits me all right.' His attention was already straying back to the canvas on the easel, a sure sign that the conversation was beginning to bore him.

'But Jude—' There were times when Kirsten could shake him. 'What if Mr Saker decides not to handle the sale after all? He might well, you know. Saker Galleries won't put their name to anything they're even slightly doubtful about.'

'So what have I lost? It makes no difference to me whether I have the drawings in a cupboard or the money in the bank.' Jude picked up his brush and added a few more strokes to his canvas, a very modernistic painting depicting a cross-section of a large house showing the luxury of the many rooms it contained and the sybaritic way of life its occupants were enjoying, completely unaware of the crumbling foundations that were threatening to bring the whole edifice crashing about their heads.

It was a very powerful painting and Kirsten could understand his absorption, then just as she thought she had lost his attention, he grinned at her over his shoulder. 'Don't look so worried, love. He'll handle the sale all right. The dealer hasn't been born who'll turn down the chance of making a fast buck, and Benet Saker's no exception. So don't let his hard luck stories pressure you into bringing my name into it—right? It's not his reputation he's worried about so much as any extra profit he might be able to squeeze out of the deal if he can cut you out.'

He really was the most exasperating man, Kirsten thought. One moment carelessly dismissing the loss of a small fortune as unimportant, and the next, showing a rather uncomfortable cynicism.

She sighed. 'Well, I expect it's too late for you to talk to Mr Saker, anyway. He'll be back in London with the drawings by now, getting the opinion of the experts.'

There was no response from Jude. His brush was moving with quick, sure strokes and he had already forgotten her existence. And that was Jude all over, utterly single-minded about his painting and as irresponsible as a child about everything else.

Climbing into the shabby old van she and Poppy used to get around to sales and to transport their stock to the weekend antique markets, Kirsten grinned to herself as she remembered some of Jude's good-natured attempts to get her into his bed. She supposed that with any other man she would have taken offence, but with Jude—somehow outraged virtue had been inappropriate. She certainly hadn't felt compelled to put an end to their friendship, not when he accepted her refusal with equal good humour.

It wasn't that Kirsten was prudish. She could hardly have reached the age of twenty-two without being aware of the permissive society, but she had never had the slightest inclination to join it. She knew Poppy had the romantic idea that she hoped to reform Jude and was holding out for marriage. She smiled to herself as she drove along the road skirting the park. As if Jude would ever make a husband! Even if she wanted to turn him into one—which she didn't.

Marriage was the last item on Kirsten's agenda. Her independence, after nearly ten years of knuckling under to her aunt's domination, had been too painfully and laboriously won for her to consider giving it up for years yet, if ever. In any case, she wasn't in love with Jude, couldn't in fact imagine there was any man who could tempt her to give up the freedom she valued so much. Poppy, being of such a romantic nature, was certain to get married one day, if not to the man she believed herself to be in love with at the moment, but Kirsten thought there was a lot to be said for being a career girl, building up her business until it rivalled Saker Galleries.

And that reminded her of her confrontation with Benet Saker that morning. She had to admit he was a very attractive man. At least, he would be if it weren't for his arrogant manner and that ruthless chin. A frisson of unease ran down her spine. She certainly wouldn't want to earn the enmity of a man with a chin like that! Today's little brush with him had been enough to show her what an implacable adversary he could be. And Aunt Gussie would like to see her married to him! Well, thank heavens this was the twentieth century and she could choose for herself whom she'd marry, or even whether she would marry at all. Just imagine escaping her aunt's domination only to fall under the thumb of a man like Benet Saker! Not in a thousand years.

She was reversing the van into the yard behind the antique shop when she saw the funny side of her grim determination not to fall in with her aunt's plans for her. Even if she had been eager to offer herself as the sacrificial lamb to her aunt's ambitions, she could hardly see Benet Saker falling meekly into line. Wealthy, successful and admittedly attractive, if he had reached the age of thirty-four without giving up his bachelor status it was because that was the way he liked it. She gave a gurgle of laughter at the very idea of Aunt Gussie being able to bully him into surrendering his bachelorhood to marry a girl he disliked. No, not even disliked. 'Our little secretary,' he had called her. He hadn't even noticed her enough to return the antipathy she felt for him. As far as he was concerned she was a faceless nobody whose very existence he had already forgotten.

All the same, Kirsten thought as she unlocked the door and started up the narrow stairs to the flat over the shop, she didn't think she would mention her meeting with Benet to Aunt Gussie. Which meant she had better not mention it to Poppy either, in case her friend's incautious tongue let something slip in Aunt Gussie's hearing. Which was a pity, she thought with a twinge of regret, because she would have enjoyed discussing Benet Saker with Poppy.

She was only halfway up the dimly lit stairway when the living room door flew open. 'You have a visitor,' Poppy hissed down at her, hanging over the banister rail, and for just a moment Kirsten feared some extra-sensory perception had brought her aunt calling. Why else would Poppy feel it necessary to warn her? But then her friend went on, 'He said he'd wait even though I told him I didn't know where you'd gone or how long you'd be.'

'He?' Kirsten ran up the last few steps. 'Who on earth is it?' she whispered.

Poppy grinned, her bright eyes full of speculation. 'See for yourself.' She pushed open the door.

'Benet!' Kirsten stopped dead on the threshold, staring at her boss in disbelief.

CHAPTER TWO

THE shock of seeing the man she had believed to be far away in London by now, looking completely at his ease in her own living room, made her forget her manners, and when she realised her familiarity in addressing her boss by his first name she corrected herself quickly in embarrassed confusion. 'I—I'm sorry. Mr Saker, I mean.'

'Benet will do.' He uncurled his length from the easy chair and stood up. 'Good evening, Kirsten. I hope you'll forgive me for dropping in like this.'

'Of—of course,' she said weakly. 'I'm sorry to have kept you waiting.'

'Your friend here has been entertaining me very well,' he assured her gravely, but there was amusement lurking in those astonishing blue eyes. It was a reaction Kirsten was used to when people saw her and Poppy together for the first time, being only five feet three and a quarter inches in her chunky-heeled boots herself, while Poppy didn't fall so very far short of Benet's own height and was lanky with it.

'Think nothing of it.' Poppy grinned irrepressibly and there was a hint of regret in her voice as she went on, 'I'll leave you two to discuss your business while I go and make some more coffee.'

The door closed behind her and for a moment Kirsten felt a surge of panic at being left alone with this man who dominated the small room so completely. She seized on Poppy's words to reassure herself. Business. Of course, that could be the only reason why he had come. There were more questions about the drawings he needed to ask before he took them back to London.

'There's something you want to know?' It came out more brusquely than she had intended, but he made her nervous, towering over her. 'Please—won't you sit down again?' she urged.

Politely he indicated that she should be seated first and then sat down opposite her, leaning forward slightly. 'Yes, there is. Kirsten, why didn't you tell me you're Gussie Douglas's niece?'

She was so taken aback by the unexpected question that she could only stutter, 'I—I assumed you knew.'

'Perhaps I should have done, but I leave the routine running of the business here to Davina, and I certainly didn't recognise you when you walked into her office this morning.' A smile tugged at the corners of his mouth. 'You've changed quite a lot from the skinny, sad-eyed little waif you were when we first met.'

'You—you remember?' Kirsten gasped in amazement, and then blushed as she realised there was frank appreciation in the eyes that were studying her confused reaction.

'It wasn't so long ago, What—six, eight years?'

'Ten. I'd just gone to live with Aunt Gussie after my parents were killed,' she corrected him faintly, and then realised that this was an admission that she remembered too.

'And your aunt? How is she?' he asked politely. 'I've neglected her shamefully these last few years.'

'V-very well, thank you,' she responded, struggling to hide her dismay. Oh help! He wasn't going to suggest visiting her while he was here, was he? The prospect of what Aunt Gussie might say or do filled her with consternation.

'At least, she was very well a few days ago when I last saw her,' she babbled in a nervous attempt at polite conversation. 'As you can see, I don't live with her at Lake House any more. I'm sorry if you think I should have told you of the connection, but it didn't occur to me. Does it make any difference?'

'I should say it does. It puts quite a different complexion on the business we have in hand.' Smiling, he relaxed back in his chair.

'Oh?' Kirsten looked at him doubtfully. 'In what way?'

'Reputations in my business often hang on knowing whom you can trust,' he said. 'Quite frankly, tempting as the offer to handle the sale of those drawings was, I was almost ready to turn it down. The typist who's only worked for the firm for a short time turns up with some unknown works by a sought-after artist—for all I knew you could have been deliberately planted at Saker Galleries for the sole purpose of working a fraud.'

'But now you can trust me—because I'm Gussie Douglas's niece?' she said sarcastically. It wasn't a case of *what* she was but *who* she was.

'I can, can't I?' Benet had fixed her with that penetrating gaze again, as if he was trying to see right into her head, as if, even though she had the right relations, his wasn't a naturally trusting nature.

This time she met his gaze levelly. 'Yes, you can, though I don't follow your reasoning.'

'You don't?' The dark eyebrows soared. 'Well, never mind. Suppose you explain to me how you drew this up.' He brought a folded sheet of paper from an inside pocket and Kirsten recognised the family tree she had drafted to trace the historical background of Jude's drawings.

'It's quite simple,' she said crisply. 'My friend gave me his mother's maiden name and her date and place of birth, together with as much of his family background as he knew. Given that starting point, it wasn't difficult to trace the family back through the public records as far as his great-grandfather, who *was* the illegitimate son of a young Tynemouth girl of humble origins, the daughter of a fisherman. The name of the baby's father was left blank in the parish register, but as you see, the date of birth was not long after Winslow Homer is thought to have returned to the States.'

'There must have been many illegitimate births in the Tynemouth area at the same period,' he challenged.

'True, but none of *their* descendants is in possession of drawings that bear Winslow Homer's signature,' she retorted. 'Of course, I realise none of this is incontrovertible proof. It merely means Winslow Homer *could* have been that child's father. But given the fact that the drawings have remained in the possession of the family, if they *are* judged by experts to be the genuine work of Winslow Homer, then surely it can be looked on as corroborative evidence?'

Benet was silent for several long moments, then he nodded, smiling. 'Very thorough and open-minded, but then I wouldn't have expected anything less from someone brought up by Gussie Douglas.'

Kirsten flushed at the compliment and Benet stretched out his long legs, looking utterly relaxed, before throwing her again by going off at another tangent. 'You're not a bit like her, you know,' he said, and she noticed his lips were twitching with suppressed amusement.

Almost against her will she found his amusement infectious. 'Thank you. I take it that *is* a compliment?'

Kirsten had every reason to be grateful to Aunt Gussie for bringing her up after her parents were killed in a road accident. Her father's sister, older than him by fifteen years, was comfortably off but unmarried, and it couldn't have been easy for her to take on the responsibility of a twelve-year-old girl whose secure and loving world had just been irrevocably shattered. Yet while Kirsten respected her aunt, she had never had the slightest desire to emulate her. 'The Iron Lady' her school-friends had called her, and from the rigid corseting that buttressed her ample figure to her steely determination to live Kirsten's life for her, the nickname suited her.

On second thoughts, Kirsten wondered ruefully, perhaps she *had* inherited some of that same steely determination, for without it she would never have broken away from her aunt's dominating influence. She could still shudder at the memory of the battle of wills a year before when she had told her aunt she was putting her small inheritance into the partnership with Poppy. And although Kirsten had won that battle, she still hadn't won the war. Aunt Gussie still hadn't given up trying to press her into the mould of dutiful and obedient niece until such time as Kirsten became the dutiful and obedient wife of the kind of man her aunt would approve of—preferably Benet Saker.

'It was meant as a compliment,' Benet smiled, his face looking almost boyish as he added mischievously, 'I don't mind admitting, Gussie Douglas can be a bit intimidating at times.'

'She intimidates *you*! But she's always approved of you,' Kirsten said unguardedly, then blushed like a livid sunset even though he could have no idea of her aunt's ludicrous dream for their joint future. 'I—I mean, she and your father have been close friends for years,' she finished lamely.

'And a very good friend she's been to him, too. Tell me, Kirsten, was it her idea that you should bring those drawings to us?'

She shook her head quickly. 'Oh no. I've never talked to Aunt Gussie about them.'

He looked surprised. 'Any reason why not?'

Kirsten felt her resentment rising at his persistent questioning, at his determination to bring her aunt into the conversation all the time, almost as if he wished it was the aunt he was dealing with and not the niece he apparently still couldn't quite trust.

'Aunt Gussie never approved of me coming into the antiques business with Poppy,' she said shortly. And her aunt certainly wouldn't have approved of Jude, she added to herself.

'But you still went ahead? Knowing your aunt, that took guts.' There was a knowing sympathy in his eyes that made her ashamed of her resentment. And then with another of those disconcerting changes of direction he said, 'So you're convinced these drawings are the genuine article and warrant the Gallery's full attribution?'

'I didn't say that.' Kirsten wasn't so naïve as to fall into that trap. 'I'm only claiming I've gone as thoroughly as I know how into their historical background and everything fits. I don't pretend to be any kind of expert on the work of Winslow Homer.'

'But my father is. His speciality was nineteenth-century American painters.' Benet was suddenly brisk and businesslike. 'That's the reason for this visit tonight. I'd like your permission to take the drawings for him to examine. I want to get Gene Deland out from the New York gallery, too—I doubt if anyone knows more about Winslow Homer than he does—and if they're both of the opinion that the work is genuine, there might be enough time to get the drawings into an important sale we're mounting in New York shortly.'

'Yes, of course you have my permission to do whatever you think best,' Kirsten agreed at once. 'I'll be the first to admit I'm a rank beginner when it comes to handling something as big as this. I wouldn't know where to start.'

'Then I'm sure you'll be glad of the chance to widen your experience by learning from two of the best experts in their field,' Benet said, rising to his feet.

Kirsten stared up at him, her green eyes very wide and startled. 'I'm sorry—I don't follow you. Surely I've played ed my part until the sale is over?'

'My dear girl, your part has hardly begun,' he said

impatiently. 'You're our only link with the owner of the drawings, the only one who can vouch for their background. You'll have to come with me.'

Kirsten was stunned. Never for one moment had she expected this. 'But—but I can't!' she gasped, springing to her feet in agitation. 'It's out of the question. There's my job, and—'

'Can't?' His eyes narrowed and his mouth compressed, his chin jutting truculently so that all traces of his earlier friendliness were wiped away. 'Let me remind you, Kirsten, that this set-up is not of *my* choosing. I would have much preferred to work directly with the vendor. It's you who are insisting on acting as the go-between and, as you'll be drawing your commission, you can hardly complain at being expected to earn it. As for your job at the gallery—Davina was arranging for a temp to stand in for you before I left, so there's no reason why you can't catch the plane with me the day after tomorrow.'

The day after tomorrow! Kirsten could only gape at him speechlessly. He hadn't come here to ask her permission to take the drawings out of the country. It had already been arranged before he even got here. He'd only come to give her her orders.

'Sorry I've been so long.' The door had opened with a rattle and Poppy backed in carrying the tray of coffee. 'Whoops! Have I chosen a bad moment?' She looked from one to the other of them as if sensing the crackling tension in the air.

'Not at all, Poppy.' Benet turned to her with an apologetic smile. 'But I'm afraid I can't stay. I've already trespassed too much on your time.' He began to move to the door and, still in a state of shock, Kirsten followed him to show him out. At the bottom of the stairs he opened the door for himself, but then he paused, looking down at her. 'You look pole-axed. Is it going to be such a penance to spend a few days in Bermuda with me, Kirsten?' he asked quizzically, then before she could find an answer, he had gone.

'Did he say Bermuda!' Poppy stood in the middle of the living room still clutching the coffee tray, her brown eyes as round as a bush-baby's.

Kirsten took the tray from her and put it down on the table. Her hand shook as she poured herself a cup and drank it thirstily, hardly noticing that it was hot enough to take the skin off her mouth, so badly did she feel in need of a restorative.

'By the look of you, you need something stronger than coffee,' Poppy commented, curiosity and concern warring in her lively dark eyes. 'Kirsten, what *is* going on? Why does he want you to go to Bermuda with him?'

'It's where Theo Saker, Benet's father, retired to when his arthritis got too bad for him to run the gallery,' Kirsten explained faintly, still with a feeling of complete unreality. 'Apparently he's an expert on nineteenth-century American artists and Benet wants him to authenticate the drawings before they go to auction. Being so crippled, of course Mr Saker can't undertake the journey here.'

'But a tropical island! Or is it sub-tropical? I've never been able to work out the difference. And with a dish like Benet Saker, too. Kirsten, isn't he just dreamy? And so tall . . .' That was always Poppy's yardstick, being not so far short of six feet herself.

'And so overbearing!' The shock was beginning to wear off, leaving a growing resentment at the way she had been dictated to. 'He didn't ask me if I wanted to go. He told me I *had* to.'

'Don't you *want* to go? I'd give my eye-teeth for the chance.'

'What? With Jeffrey due home from Brussels any day now?' Kirsten couldn't help teasing at Poppy's dreamy expression. 'I thought you were wildly in love with him.'

'Yes, well, I am, but it's very unsettling being so unsure

if he feels the same way about me. I mean, he did jump at the offer of that job in Brussels, didn't he? And he never suggested we got engaged before he went. I wouldn't mind having a man like Benet Saker in reserve if Jeffrey's finding the continental ladies more fascinating than me,' Poppy smiled irrepressibly. 'Oh—' A look of rueful understanding crossed her face. 'I suppose you're worried about what Jude will say to your going off with another man like that.'

'Of course I'm not. Don't be silly.' Kirsten's voice was unusually sharp and her cup rattled against the saucer as she put it down. 'It's nothing to do with Jude where I go or with whom—except, in this case, in a purely business sense. I'll be going there on his behalf, don't forget. It was *his* idea to have his name kept out of the negotiations.'

Poppy shrugged. 'If you say so. Then I can't imagine why you're not more excited about the chance of a trip like that,' she said frankly. 'Think of it, Kirsten. All that lovely sunshine, those blue seas and white beaches fringed with palm trees . . . *and* a man as dishy as Benet Saker.'

Kirsten *was* thinking about it, and with the first stirrings of excitement. But she was determined not to let Poppy's imagination—or her own—run away with them both. 'It isn't going to be a pleasure trip,' she reminded her friend. 'It'll be purely business.'

'Phooey!' Poppy was openly disbelieving. 'Benet Saker didn't strike me as the kind of man who doesn't know how to enjoy himself when the opportunity arises, so don't try to pretend he's going to take you all that way without finding the time to show you some of the sights while you're there, or that you won't enjoy seeing them with him. What have you got in your veins, for heaven's sake? Red blood or iced water?'

Something flickered along Kirsten's nerve ends and she found she was remembering the look in Benet's eyes when he had asked her if spending a few days in Bermuda with him was going to be such a penance. It had been an odd look, almost as if he was taking up a challenge, and it had made her heart flutter. But remembering it now, when his disturbing presence was gone, she supposed it was only natural that he should have been surprised and rather nettled at her dismayed reaction to his invitation—if invitation it could be called. As Poppy had so rightly implied, most girls would have jumped for joy at the offer of an all-expenses-paid trip to Bermuda, and in the company of such an attractive man, too. She couldn't believe Benet was unaware of his attractions so her reluctance must have been a new experience for him.

And if she was honest, Kirsten knew she could have been very excited about it herself, if only it hadn't been for Aunt Gussie and her weird fantasy. She groaned inwardly. There would be no holding her aunt's ambitious dreams when she heard about this! It would be bad enough having Aunt Gussie know she had at last met Benet Saker, but when she learned they were flying out to Bermuda together . . . Kirsten wouldn't be surprised if she didn't start making arrangements for the wedding!

An even worse possibility occurred to her, making the scorching colour run up her neck and into her face. Suppose when Aunt Gussie heard about the trip she contacted Benet at the gallery to pass on some message for his father, and suppose she betrayed the way her mind was working! Kirsten knew very well her aunt was capable of such blundering tactlessness. That Benet Saker should ever get the breath of a suspicion of what Aunt Gussie planned for them both made Kirsten cringe.

'What are you looking so worried about now?' Poppy demanded in exasperation.

Kirsten blinked at her, dragged back from her appalling thoughts. 'I—I was just wondering what on earth I could take with me to wear,' she prevaricated.

'Gosh, yes! Your wardrobe's hardly jet-set class, is it?

Come on, let's see how we can fit you out between us.'
Poppy hustled her into the bedroom and began to drag
clothes from the cupboard, and Kirsten was too preoccupied to see the funny side of the suggestion that she might
be able to make use of anything belonging to Poppy when
her friend was at least eight inches taller than she was.

Could she possibly make this trip without telling Aunt
Gussie? She chewed her bottom lip and, as Poppy chat-
tered on, tried to assess the likelihood of her finding out
from any other source. Her aunt might pay an unexpected
visit to the flat while she was away, especially as Kirsten
hadn't been to see her for a week or so. But if she dropped
into Lake House tomorrow night, Kirsten thought, that
would give her a few days' breathing space before her aunt
felt impelled to keep tabs on her again. And if her aunt *did*
call at the flat while Kirsten was away, she could always
warn Poppy not to tell her where she had gone or with
whom.

There was Davina, of course. She would almost certainly mention the trip if the two women should happen to
meet. But while they knew each other quite well, they
weren't exactly friends. And Benet had said it was only
going to be for a few days. Her aunt would be furious at
being kept in the dark, but if she *did* come to hear about it
later, it wouldn't matter as long as Benet was safely back in
London.

Kirsten felt so much better having come to her decision
and she was able to turn her attention to her sadly
inadequate wardrobe. All she seemed to possess were
jeans and sweaters or the prim little dresses she wore to
work at the gallery. And all Poppy could lend her was a
couple of skimpy bikinis Kirsten doubted if she would
have the courage to wear.

It was only as she lay in bed that night that she
remembered her passport was still at Lake House. She
groaned inwardly. This simple business trip seemed to be

fraught with obstacles. Perhaps she would be able to search out her passport without her aunt knowing. And if that proved impossible she would just have to make up a convincing story. She punched her pillow crossly. She felt guilty enough deceiving her aunt by the sin of omission, but to compound the sin by actually having to tell lies made her feel deeply guilty.

As Kirsten pushed open the door of the gallery the next morning she almost cannoned into Benet on his way out. He stopped, his eyebrows lifted in surprise. 'What are you doing here?'

Kirsten stared at him blankly. 'I've come to work, of course.'

'But my dear girl we'll be leaving at crack of dawn tomorrow to get to the airport. There must be a thousand and one things you have to do before then.' He had taken her arm and was walking her out to the pavement. 'No one expected you to work today.'

'You just expected me to be a mind-reader, I suppose,' Kirsten retorted.

He threw her a keen glance, half irritated, half amused. 'Davina's already showing your stand-in the ropes so you can take the day off with a clear conscience. I was on my way to see you, actually. I forgot to check with you last night that you have an up-to-date passport.'

By this time Kirsten was so flustered she said unguardedly, 'Oh yes, but it's still at Lake House. I'm going to pick it up this evening.'

'Then that's one chore we can get out of the way right now. I'll run you over.' He steered her towards the gleaming brown sporty Jaguar car parked at the kerb.

'No!' She planted her feet firmly on the pavement, resisting the pressure on her arm. 'There's no need for you to take so much trouble,' she blurted out breathlessly. 'If I don't have to work today I can run myself over there in the van.'

'No trouble.' One hand was still gripping her arm while the other opened the passenger door. 'I was going to see your aunt anyway, to ask her permission to carry you off to Bermuda.'

Kirsten went hot and then cold. He couldn't. There was no way she could let him get within a mile of Aunt Gussie! She had to stop him and she had to do it without telling him why. 'I'm over twenty-one. I don't have to ask her permission,' she snapped, her anxiety making her sound aggressive.

'All right, I'll rephrase it.' She was aware of the censure in the glance that flicked over her. 'We'll go and ask if she minds. Or didn't she manage to instil any manners into you during those twenty-one years?'

Kirsten's face burned. 'I can tell her myself. There's no need for you to go, too.'

He appeared to be grinding his teeth together. 'No, but I'm going all the same. As I said last night, I've neglected your aunt disgracefully these last few years. And, as you have to pick up your passport from there, it seems logical for us to go together. So will you stop throwing tantrums and get in?'

'Don't treat me like a child,' she said angrily.

'Don't behave like one.' He thrust her into the car and slammed the door.

As he walked round the front of the car to get into the driving seat her fingers fumbled for the door handle, but then she slumped back into her seat in defeat. If he was going to see Aunt Gussie anyway, there was no point in her running away. Her plan to keep her aunt in the dark about her trip was now blown. Benet was determined to ask her if she minded the two of them going off to Bermuda together. Minded! Aunt Gussie would be in her seventh heaven. Kirsten felt hot and prickly all over with apprehension at the conclusions she just *knew* her aunt would jump to.

She stared blindly in front of her as the car wove through the traffic then picked up speed as the town was left behind. For heaven's sake, couldn't Benet have had the wit to realise she had a very good reason for not wanting him to see Aunt Gussie? Obviously not. They were a good pair—Benet was every bit as autocratic and overbearing as her aunt when it came to getting his own way.

She wiped damp palms against her skirt. Should she prepare him for what he was in for? She tried to formulate the words in her mind. 'Perhaps I should warn you, Benet, that my aunt has this silly fixation about you and me falling in love and getting married. Yes, ridiculous isn't it? You mustn't take any notice. I don't.' She would say it in a light, laughing voice . . .

But her mouth was dry and she was so tense that when she began, 'Perhaps—' it came out as a hoarse croak and she bit it off quickly.

'I'm sorry?' Benet glanced at her questioningly.

'Nothing,' she muttered. It was too late anyway. The car was already turning into the drive that dipped steeply down into the green bowl of land cradling the lake at the bottom and the creamy stone house on the rising ground beyond. She could only hope her aunt wouldn't be at home.

It was a vain hope. The car had hardly stopped before the front door opened and Aunt Gussie, her well-corseted figure clad in smart tweeds, her iron-grey hair lying in disciplined waves against her head, was hurrying down the steps.

'Benet—my dear boy! I can hardly believe my eyes.'

Her hand arrested on the handle of the car door, Kirsten watched the spectacle of her aunt submitting to Benet's enthusiastic hug, lifting a cheek flushed with pleasure for his kiss. It gave her a peculiarly painful feeling in her chest, because in all the years she had lived with her aunt, never once had *she* been the recipient of such a show of affection.

'Is that a reproach for neglecting you so long?' Benet's smile was wry as he held Aunt Gussie at arm's length. 'If it is, I deserve it.'

'I understand how busy you've been,' she said forgivingly. 'Your father told me in his letters the problems you've had setting up the New York gallery. Is everything going smoothly there now? Come inside, my dear boy, and tell me all about it.'

For a moment Kirsten thought—hoped—he'd forgotten her, but then he turned back and opened the car door. 'Are you going to skulk in here all day?' There was a censorious note in his voice as she hastily climbed out.

'Kirsten!' There was no mistaking her aunt's astonishment, or the speculative gleam in her eyes as she looked first at her niece and then at Benet. She offered a powdered cheek which Kirsten brushed with her own, the awareness of what was going on in her aunt's mind making her stiff with embarrassment. Her aunt turned back to Benet at once and Kirsten followed the two of them into the house reluctantly.

'You can ask Mrs Pattinson if she'll be good enough to make us some coffee, Kirsten,' her aunt said over her shoulder as she ushered Benet into the sitting room, and it was with a feeling of relief that Kirsten hurried down the hall to the kitchen. The kitchen had always been the one place in her aunt's house where she felt the most at ease and the brisk ministrations of Mrs Pattinson who ruled there the nearest she had come to being mothered since her own mother's death.

'Miss Kirsten! How did *you* get here at this time of day? In that death-trap of an old van of yours, I suppose.' The elderly lady's greeting was a mixture of pleasure and reproof.

'Not today, Patti, I came in style.' She hugged the

housekeeper then grimaced wryly: 'Benet Saker brought me.'

'Mr Benet's come too?' All trace of reproof was erased from Patti's lined face. 'Oh, your aunt *will* be pleased. She hasn't seen him since her last trip to London and that's ages ago.'

Sitting on the corner of the kitchen table swinging her legs and watching the housekeeper spooning coffee into the filter, Kirsten couldn't help contrasting her aunt's habitual stiffness to the way she unbent to greet Benet.

'She's very fond of him, isn't she?' she said at last, an unconscious note of wistfulness in her voice.

'Oh ay, she's always looked on him as a son, ever since he was left motherless as a toddler.' Patti paused as she set out the porcelain cups on the silver tray. 'I think there was a time when she expected she *would* be his mother. His stepmother, anyway,' she went on reflectively.

'She was going to *marry* Theo Saker!' Kirsten stared at her in astonishment. She tried in vain to stretch her imagination to visualise her domineering aunt as an affectionate wife and mother. 'So what happened? Why didn't she?'

'I reckon Mr Theo'd had enough of marriage by then,' Patti said cryptically. 'And I've no business to be gossiping about it now.' She resumed setting out the coffee tray.

If Aunt Gussie *had* married Theo Saker, that would have made Benet and herself kind of related, Kirsten supposed, still struggling to reconcile the picture of the aunt she knew with this surprising information. Perhaps if her aunt had gained her heart's desire, Kirsten's own life might have been less regimented, less lacking in warmth and affection.

'I suppose if she'd always fancied Benet as a son, finding herself suddenly responsible for me must have been a poor substitute,' she said ruefully.

Patti's perceptive glance contained awareness of the years of rebuff, the lonely adolescent's yearning for affection. 'Your aunt was always possessive of her men folk,' she said gruffly. 'And she never did get on with your mother. She always said as your ma was sly.'

Kirsten slid off the table, her fists clenched in outraged protest. 'My mother was *not* sly!' She was adult enough now to realise her memories of the first twelve years of her life were somewhat idealised, that it couldn't always have been sunshine and laughter as she remembered. But her mother's directness, her bubbling gaiety was something she *did* remember clearly.

'I never said she was.' Patti switched off the coffee filter. 'I said your aunt thought so, getting your pa to marry her on the quiet. But I reckon they both knew what they were doing. If they hadn't done it first and told her after, she'd have found some way to stop it.'

So Aunt Gussie had tried to run her father's life too! She had tried to stop her parents' marriage. But Mother had been too clever for her. Oh yes, Kirsten realised that the clandestine marriage must have been her mother's doing. Her gentle, peace-loving father would never have had the will to stand out against his strong-minded sister.

'I never knew,' she said thoughtfully. 'It explains a lot. If Aunt Gussie disliked my mother so much, I suppose it's not surprising she could never bring herself to care for me.'

Patti tut-tutted crossly. 'I don't know what got into me, raking all that up now. It's all water under the bridge, anyway. And she took you in, didn't she? Your aunt always had a strong sense of duty.'

Kirsten picked up the tray. It was chilling to know your only relative saw you merely as a duty.

When she carried the coffee through to the sitting room the subject of conversation was still the opening of Sakers New York gallery. Kirsten put the tray down and served the coffee without interrupting, black for Benet because that was how he had requested it yesterday at the gallery, and with a generous helping of cream and sugar for her aunt. Her own cup she took to a small chair on the fringe of the stiffly arranged group, her eyes drawn unwillingly to Benet, perfectly at his ease on one of the sofas.

Kirsten had always found this room particularly intimidating. Until she was sixteen she hadn't been allowed inside its door in case sticky finger marks or a careless kick should mar its elegance. And it *was* elegant, she supposed, high-ceilinged and well proportioned with wide, south facing windows. But the blinds were almost always drawn to keep the sun off the furnishings: walls hung with pale oyster silk, the two deep sofas and all the chairs upholstered in a matching oyster and pink brocade. Hothouse carnations stood to attention in a silver vase and no speck of dust was ever allowed to dull the sheen of the well-polished occasional tables that reflected the dainty porcelain figures her aunt collected. It always put Kirsten in mind of a room in a stately home, meant to be looked at and admired but never lived in. There wasn't a book to be seen, not even a magazine or newspaper let alone a bundle of knitting hastily thrust beneath one of those plump, brocade cushions.

And yet a house this size was surely built as a family home, she thought idly, meant to be over-run with children. She could just picture it: the sash windows opened wide to let in the sun and scents from the garden; a bunch of wild flowers, picked with the delight of discovery, thrust into a pot and a small red-headed girl trying to capture them in watercolours with no one to fly into a rage if the water got spilt and marked the polish; an older girl curled up in the window-seat with a book with no one scolding at feet on the cushions; a small boy riding astride the back of the sofa with no one worrying about spoiling the hard-wearing chintz covers; and another gambolling with a pet dog on the hearth-rug with no one complaining about dog hairs and scratched furniture. She sighed.

'Kirsten!' Coming out of her daydream she was suddenly aware that both Benet and her aunt were looking at her as if expecting an answer.

'I—I'm sorry—' She jumped up, setting her coffee cup down so jarringly on the low table she spilled some of the contents on to the polished surface. Without thinking she surreptitiously dragged the cuff of her jacket over the spill then glanced up guiltily. Her aunt had blessedly turned away to apologise for her niece's inattention, but then her face flamed when she realised Benet had seen her childish action.

He stood up and reached for the coffee pot. 'Let me refill your cup, Gussie, and leave Kirsten to her daydreams. I won't have any more, thank you. I have a lot to do before we leave tomorrow.' He replaced the coffee pot on the tray and glanced at Kirsten mockingly. 'I know Kirsten thinks herself too grown up now to have to ask your permission, but I would prefer to have your blessing on taking her to Bermuda with me tomorrow.'

'You're taking Kirsten to meet your father! Oh, my dear boy!' Aunt Gussie lumbered to her feet to grasp his hands, her face pink and beaming. 'Of course you have my blessing, Benet, and I know you'll have your father's too. It's always been our dearest wish that you and Kirsten—'

'Aunt Gussie!' Kirsten broke in desperately to stop the embarrassing flow. Stealing a glance at Benet, she was mortified to see the stunned incredulity on his face at her aunt's gushing reaction to his innocent request.

But before she could put in another word of protest Benet was saying coldly, 'I don't know what Kirsten's been telling you about this trip, Gussie, but I do assure you it's purely business that's taking us to see my father.'

The derisive tone of his voice stung while the accusation in his eyes pinned Kirsten to her chair. She had expected this visit to her aunt to be embarrassing, but she hadn't bargained on being so utterly humiliated. He thought she was chasing him! He actually thought she had misled her aunt about the nature of their relationship and had enlisted her aid in order to trap him!

Slowly, as the murmur of their continued conversation passed over her bowed head unheard, a white-hot anger grew out of her humiliation. How dared he? How dared he assume *she* had put the ludicrous idea into her aunt's head? The arrogance of the man! Had she given him the slightest reason to suspect she had designs on him? On the contrary, she had made her reluctance to accompany him to Bermuda quite plain from the outset.

When at last her seething resentment allowed her to take note of the conversation, her aunt was complacently giving Benet messages to relay to his father. He didn't as much as glance in her direction again until he had moved towards the door, and then the command in his clipped, 'Kirsten?' almost had her leaping obediently to her feet.

Almost, but not quite. 'I'll make my own way back to town, thank you,' she said stonily, gripping the sides of her chair.

'My dear girl, haven't we just said you and I will have to spend the rest of the day shopping?' Aunt Gussie did nothing to hide her irritation. 'If you can't pay attention to your elders and betters, at least show a little civility and see Benet out.'

'It'll be a pleasure,' Kirsten ground out under her breath, wishing she could be showing him out of her life for good.

Her chin high, her back ramrod straight, she swept past him as he held open the door, stalking along the hall in front of him, preceding him out of the front door and down the steps. She had reached the bottom when a hard hand on her shoulder spun her round.

'Now let's get things straight before we start, Kirsten.'

Benet towered over her threateningly, the grip on her shoulder designed to intimidate.

Well, she wasn't going to let him intimidate her. Clenching her teeth at the uncaring pain he was inflicting, she twisted sharply, knocking his hand away with furious force. 'Yes, do let's get things straight,' she flung at him, her green eyes sparking with temper. 'I resent your assumption that *I* was responsible for my aunt jumping to the wrong conclusion about the reason for this trip to Bermuda. If you were embarrassed by it, how do you think *I* felt?'

'I don't deny your embarrassment. Perhaps you should have remembered that your aunt had no subtlety when you poured out your hopes to her.' He looked so sure of himself, so dismissive, that Kirsten was enraged.

'My God, but you love yourself, don't you!' Her hands clenched and she longed to wipe the self-satisfied look from his arrogant face. 'For your information I haven't seen or spoken to my aunt for nearly two weeks until this morning, and if you hadn't been so puffed up with conceit you might have noticed how surprised she was when we arrived here together.'

He frowned, his eyes narrowing. '*Somebody* put the idea into her head, and it certainly wasn't me.'

'No?' Kirsten jeered. 'You were the one who insisted on our coming here to ask her blessing on the trip, remember. I had no intention of telling her we'd even met, let alone that you had twisted my arm to accompany you to Bermuda. I've never subscribed to my aunt's fantasies and I refuse to be held responsible for them.'

'Fantasies?' A look of distaste crossed his face. 'Are you trying to tell me Gussie thought up this matchmaking idea for herself? But it's—'

'Ludicrous?' Kirsten finished for him, her green eyes flashing beneath the shining copper halo of her hair. 'At least that's one thing we agree on. I've enjoyed my independence since I moved into the flat with Poppy. When—*if* I ever feel inclined to lose it to some man, it certainly won't be to one of my aunt's choosing.'

'You don't believe in pulling your punches, do you?'

Kirsten's eyes wavered under his gaze. Maybe she had been blunt, blunt to the point of rudeness. But was it only his height that gave the impression he was looking down his nose at her? She was quick to notice he didn't attempt an apology.

Her chin came up again. 'You did say you wanted to get things straight and I merely wanted to assure you there was no danger whatever of my making a nuisance of myself by getting starry-eyed over you. I thought you'd be relieved, Mr Saker, to learn you don't appeal to me at all. Good day.'

She turned on her heel and stalked back into the house, feeling his eyes boring into her at every step. But she was determined not to look round, and so she missed the wry amusement that curled his mouth and the speculative gleam in his eyes.

CHAPTER THREE

WINGING high over the Atlantic, Kirsten still found it difficult to believe she really was on her way to Bermuda. Ever since that humiliating confrontation with Benet Saker the previous morning she had been expecting a call from him to tell her the trip was off, and yet here she was in the luxurious first-class section of the aircraft, very much aware of the relaxed figure beside her.

Benet had reclined his seat and was asleep, but Kirsten was too tense even to close her eyes, a nervous hand from time to time smoothing the fine pleats of her lovely new moss-green linen suit, every restless movement making her conscious of the sensuous feel of the pure silk shirt against her skin.

When she had got back into the house yesterday morning it had been to find her aunt coming downstairs wearing a hat and pulling on her gloves.

'I do wish you could have given me more time, Kirsten,' she said irritably, picking up her car keys from the copper bowl on the elaborately carved side-table in the hall.

'Time? Time for what?' Still seething at Benet Saker's conceited arrogance, Kirsten stared at her blankly.

'Time to fit you out with the kind of wardrobe that won't disgrace me, of course. What we really need is a day in London, but—' Her aunt veered to the back of the hall and opened the door into the kitchen. 'I'm going out, Mrs Pattinson, and I shan't be back to lunch. And just make sure Betts doesn't sit around drinking tea until he's finished clipping that yew hedge.'

She closed the door with a snap and bore down on Kirsten again, frowning critically. 'You could certainly do with a little London polish, but I suppose we'll have to make the best of what the local shops can provide.'

She couldn't *still* be deluding herself about this visit to Bermuda, could she, Kirsten wondered in amazement. If the whole thing wasn't so embarrassing it would be funny.

'Aunt Gussie, weren't you listening? Surely Benet made it absolutely clear there is nothing to this trip beyond business?' Only too humiliatingly clear, she added to herself with an inward wince. 'I'll only be there for a day or two so what's the point in wasting time and money buying me new clothes?'

'Oh, I realise now I jumped a little too precipitately to conclusions,' Aunt Gussie said calmly, pausing before the mirror to tug her felt hat more firmly over the grey, tramline waves. 'Not that there's any real harm done. At least I've put the idea into his head now. The rest is up to you. And that's why it's important to turn you out smartly. You're not going to attract a man like Benet dressed as you are, like a small-town nobody.'

Kirsten was speechless. She knew her greatest weapon in counteracting her aunt's foolishness was laughter, and had Aunt Gussie's ambitions for her sprung from genuine affection, she might have been able to laugh them off. But she knew there was no affection behind the blind persistence and she could only put it down to her aunt's determination to have her own way regardless of anyone else's feelings.

'I *am* a small-town nobody,' she retaliated sharply. 'And no way is Benet Saker going to look at me, whatever fine feathers you deck me out in. I don't *want* to attract him anyway. I find him arrogant and pompous and—and totally obnoxious!'

Through the mirror she saw her aunt's mouth tighten. 'You always were the most difficult girl in the world to help, Kirsten. Ungrateful . . . rebellious . . .'

Kirsten's fair skin flushed at the accusation that had so

often been levelled at her. 'I'm not ungrateful, Aunt Gussie,' she denied. 'You've done a lot for me, given me a home and a good education, and I really do appreciate it.'

'You're my niece. It was no more than my duty,' her aunt said tightly.

Kirsten flinched at the reminder that she had been nothing more than a tiresome duty. She would willingly have settled for far fewer material advantages in exchange for a little warmth and affection. It wasn't that her aunt wasn't capable of showing affection as Kirsten had sometimes supposed. Her greeting of Benet Saker had shown a warmth in their relationship that Kirsten had envied.

'I *am* grateful,' she reiterated quietly, 'but don't you consider your duty done now, Aunt Gussie? You've provided me with the means of earning my own living.'

'If you're content that you should remain a little typist for the rest of your days, I'm not. I won't consider my duty done until I have you comfortably married. Oh, at one time it wouldn't have been so important to me. I expected to be able to leave you comfortably off after I'm gone, but with inflation—' She turned, shrugging, from the mirror. 'I hadn't intended to tell you this but—if it's the only way I can make you see sense . . . In order to keep up my standard of living I've had to come to an arrangement with an insurance company. They provide an income that will keep me very comfortably for the rest of my days, but on my death, that income will cease and Lake House will become the property of the insurance company.'

Kirsten was embarrassed by these disclosures, feeling Aunt Gussie's financial affairs were nothing to do with her, but when her aunt went on, 'Your marriage to Benet will salve my conscience,' the girl gasped.

'You—you want me to marry Benet Saker for *money*? But even if he was willing, that's—that's dishonest!'

The expression in her aunt's eyes was one of cold dislike. 'I never cared for your mother, Kirsten, but there are times when I could wish you were more like her and less like your father. *He* could never see what was good for him either. Far from being dishonest, it's very sensible to look for security in marriage. Such marriages stand far more chance of success than so-called love matches if the divorce statistics are anything to go by.'

Kirsten felt chilled. She had never been in love, but she could imagine what it might be like, and she was sure she could never give up her independence for anything less. It would never be enough for her to settle for a man she thought she might be able to live with, however much security he could offer. She would only marry if she found a man she couldn't live without.

'And just what is Benet supposed to get out of this marriage?' she asked, her voice heavy with an irony that was lost on her aunt.

'A wife who has been carefully brought up to fill her position adequately and the knowledge that he'll be pleasing both me and his father,' Aunt Gussie said confidently. 'Now come along, do. We've wasted too much time as it is.'

Kirsten opened her mouth to protest further but realised it would be as useless as trying to stop an armoured tank with a broom. She had done her best to point out the fatal flaw in her aunt's plans, she thought philosophically as she climbed into the passenger seat of the sedate black Rover. Even if Kirsten herself had been willing to go along with such an outrageous scheme, it took two to make a marriage. But if Aunt Gussie was determined to believe that a new dress was going to change her small-town niece into the kind of creature Benet Saker was going to lose his head over, then Kirsten felt she need have no more conscience about accepting it. Time alone would prove to her aunt how foolishly impossible her hopes were.

Aunt Gussie drove as she did everything else, as if she expected everyone else to defer to her. Neither did it trouble her in the least that she might be causing an obstruction when she parked right outside the best store the town boasted. And once inside the store she demanded instant attention, which she got as soon as it became apparent that, rather than the one or two new dresses Kirsten had reluctantly prepared herself to accept, her aunt made it clear she was to be re-equipped from the skin out; lacy underwear and filmy tights, a couple of diaphanous nighties and matching negligees, crisp cotton sundresses and slinky evening gowns, a fine linen suit for travelling and contrasting silk shirt, casual wear, shoes and sandals.

'Aunt Gussie, I can't possibly let you buy me all this,' Kirsten remonstrated as the purchases began to pile up, every new one adding to her sense of obligation and deepening her guilt because she knew in no way could she repay this investment as her aunt wanted. 'You—you know you can't afford it.' Remembering her aunt's admission of how she had had to rearrange her affairs she seized on the one objection she thought would carry some weight.

'Let me be the judge of what I can afford, Kirsten,' her aunt said stiffly from the gilt chair where she sat directing operations. 'If you're really concerned, then see to it that I haven't wasted my money.'

'You *are* wasting it,' she insisted wretchedly, but she was ignored as Aunt Gussie demanded that the assistant should show them some beachwear next.

Biting her lip as she was hustled back into the changing room by a sales girl only too eager to swell her commission even further, Kirsten struggled with the warring emotions of anger, frustration and helplessness. If fitting her out with an expensive new wardrobe had been just a generous gesture on her aunt's part to enable her to enjoy the unexpected chance of a trip to Bermuda, she could have accepted it with gratitude. It was the strings attached to the gift that made her position untenable. She felt trapped, obligated to her aunt to attempt something her common sense told her was impossible, something her every instinct flinched from in distaste—the cold-blooded seduction of a rich man into marriage.

'Your trousseau, is it?' the assistant asked curiously as she displayed a selection of the scantiest bikinis Kirsten had ever seen.

'Oh no, nothing like that.' Kirsten shook her head quickly, feeling near to hysteria. If only Benet Saker could have been witness to her aunt's conversation since he left them this morning! Perhaps then he wouldn't be so all-fire quick to assume his old friend Gussie Douglas could do no wrong. His immediate assumption that it must have been Kirsten herself who had put the idea into her aunt's head still rankled like a burr under her skin.

'It's just a holiday, then?' The young assistant couldn't hide her envy.

'Just a holiday,' Kirsten agreed, deciding there was no point in arguing. She eyed the bikinis warily. 'Don't you have anything a bit less . . . I think I'd feel more comfortable in a one-piece suit.'

'Oh, but your aunt insisted on something glamorous, and they don't come more glamorous than this,' the girl coaxed, holding up what was little more than four tiny triangles held together with cords in a shiny gold material.

'It—it's indecent!' Kirsten gasped a minute or two later as she looked at her reflection in the mirror.

'It's gorgeous!' the girl laughed. 'You've got curves in all the right places. Even without a tan that'll fetch the men like bees round honey.'

Kirsten was about to retort that she didn't want to fetch the men—least of all one particular man—but somehow the words were never spoken. Into her mind sprang the image of Benet Saker as he had towered over her outside Lake House, so superior, so contemptuously dismissive. If anything might find a chink in that superior armour of his, an outfit like this might, she found herself thinking.

Kirsten had never had the time or the interest to pay much attention to what she looked like, but now she studied herself from all angles. Even with her winter-pale skin the daring bikini showed off a figure no girl need feel ashamed of, the supple gold fabric clinging to the firm, swelling mounds of her breasts, the gold cords across her curving hips giving a flattering length to her legs. And, given an idyllic setting like Bermuda, white sands, blue seas, golden sunshine, was it so impossible to imagine Benet Saker finding her just a little bit attractive?

Why not? Her pointed chin tilted a fraction higher and her green eyes sparkled with a challenge. Why not make good use of all these beautiful trappings Aunt Gussie was decking her out in? Oh, not to try to beguile a proposal from him. That was a non-starter, however much her aunt chose to delude herself. Benet Saker had far too high an opinion of his own value ever to fall for that. But oh, the pleasure she would get from having him lust after her just a little, and then to freeze him off with the same icy contempt he had shown towards her . . .

This time she agreed without a murmur of protest to the purchase of the gold bikini as well as one in almond green and another in black and a skimpy hip-length beach wrap to go over them. And she steeled herself against a stab of conscience when her aunt said complacently, 'I'm glad you're beginning to see a little sense at last, Kirsten,' obviously assuming the lack of argument signalled a more amenable state of mind on her niece's part.

It wasn't as if anyone would get hurt, Kirsten told herself. Aunt Gussie's foolish hopes were doomed to disappointment anyway, and there was no danger of damaging Benet's ego. And it wasn't as if either of them was in the least concerned with Kirsten's feelings.

'But why the sudden generosity?' Poppy demanded

later that afternoon as she drooled over the new finery. She had been in their shop when the black Rover had pulled up outside and she had immediately followed the laden Kirsten up to the flat. 'Your aunt's never given you more than a small bottle of perfume at birthdays and Christmas since I've known you.'

Kirsten sighed ruefully and gave her an edited version of her aunt's sudden burst of matchmaking. She expected her friend to echo her own view, that such an idea was ludicrous, but Poppy whistled and her eyes widened.

'Wow! You lucky thing. So you could beat me to the altar yet.'

'Oh Poppy, don't *you* start!' Kirsten laughed, but irritation wasn't far behind. 'I've no intention of trying to make Aunt Gussie's fantasies come true. I don't want to marry anyone, and certainly not a man as full of himself as Benet Saker.'

'You don't?' Poppy flung her lanky frame into the one chair that wasn't already piled high with the contents of Kirsten's parcels and gazed up at her curiously. 'Don't you fancy him at all then? He's very attractive, Kirsten, and sexy.'

Try as she would, Kirsten couldn't quite banish the memory of the sheer masculine virility that had emanated from him as he had gripped her shoulders so painfully. Luckily, she could also remember the humiliation of being accused of giving Aunt Gussie the wrong idea about their relationship.

'And he knows it,' she retorted swiftly. 'You don't imagine a man with *his* outsize conceit is going to look at an ordinary little nobody like me, do you? Even if I wanted him to,' she hastened to add.

'Don't undersell yourself, Kirsten. You're quite a sexy little number yourself, or you could be if you didn't keep trying to convince yourself you only want a career. And with all these gorgeous new clothes to flaunt yourself in—all I can say is, I only wish I'd got someone like Aunt Gussie in *my* corner.' Poppy's animated face was suddenly wistful. 'Jeffrey phoned today,' she went on with an unusual diffidence. 'To tell me he'd be here by the end of the week.'

'But that's marvellous!' Kirsten enthused, wondering at her friend's lack of excitement.

'Only for a fortnight's leave, though. He's going back again after—Still, he did call me all the way from Brussels, and he *did* talk for ages and it must have cost a bomb. That has to mean something, doesn't it?' She looked at Kirsten with naked appeal in her eyes.

'You really do love him, don't you?' Kirsten said softly, and Poppy nodded.

'I know I made light of it, but I really was dreadfully hurt when he took this job abroad and went off without trying to settle anything between us. Oh, he's written regularly, but his letters never tell me how he feels about me. I thought I'd get over wanting him so much, but it's been three months now and I'm missing him more than ever.'

Kirsten squeezed her hand as a sympathetic lump rose in her throat. 'The fact that he wants to come back and spend his leave with you is a good sign, don't you think?' she said encouragingly.

Poor Poppy. So falling in love wasn't all joy and happiness, not if you couldn't be sure that that love was returned. But even so, it made Kirsten even more determined not to give her aunt the slightest encouragement in her mercenary schemes.

'Poppy, will you do me a favour?' she blurted out, still following her own train of thought. 'I don't suppose she *will* come near you, but if you *do* see my aunt while I'm away, spin her some yarn about my being heavily involved with some boy-friend, will you?'

'It really does bother you then, her trying to pair you off

with Benet Saker? I think you're nuts but—' She grinned.
'Okay, if that's how you want to play it. Who do you
suggest? Jude Ofield?'

Kirsten hesitated. She had promised to keep Jude's
name out of things, but then her aunt wasn't concerned
with the business of the drawings. 'If you like. It doesn't
really matter whose name you use,' she agreed carelessly.
'At least it might prepare her for the inevitable disappointment.'

Of course, Benet Saker might still solve the problem for
her by calling off the trip . . . But by the following morning
there had been no word from him and even the elegance of
her new moss-green suit was no armour against the swarm
of butterflies in her stomach. She was beginning to see her
resolve to puncture his self-esteem for what it really was, a
bit of childish wishful thinking. Even if she got the chance
to wear that very revealing bikini—which she very much
doubted—how could she ever have imagined it would
affect him in the slightest? She only had to think about the
beautiful and sophisticated women he must be accus-
tomed to escorting around London, those he must have
shared holidays with in the past, to cut herself down to
size. And after the way she had spoken to him yesterday,
Benet was going to be even more coldly superior, even
more unapproachable and Kirsten could only hope to grit
her teeth and ride out what promised to be a very uncomfortable few days.

But so far it hadn't been at all uncomfortable, she
thought, gazing down at the cotton wool clouds far below
the wing-tips of the plane. That surprised her and, because
it was so unexpected, she felt uneasy. When Benet had
called to collect her, the anger of the morning before had
disappeared to be replaced with a teasing charm that had
left her confused and feeling rather foolish at her own
rather truculent greeting. All the way to Heathrow Airport he had kept up an easy flow of conversation and

gradually her own replies had become less guarded as she relaxed.

Being a seasoned traveller, he had steered her effortlessly through the formalities and as they waited for their flight to be called she became aware of the appreciative and even covetous glances he was drawing from several female passengers. Not that Benet seemed to notice. All his attention seemed to be centred on Kirsten herself, ordering her coffee, buying her magazines to while away the tedium of the flight.

While the knowledge that she was the envy of women far prettier and more sophisticated than herself was heady, Kirsten almost wished he wouldn't. She was beginning to find his charm every bit as disturbing as his former hostility, if in a very different way. She knew she ought to be thankful that he had decided to behave like a normal civilised person, but she couldn't help wondering *why* he was suddenly putting himself out to please her.

Surely her outspoken estimate of his character yesterday hadn't hit home? Could it be that he was trying to rectify her unflattering opinion of him? She shrugged away the thought as not worthy of her consideration. Benet Saker didn't care tuppence what she thought of his character. Perhaps then, after sleeping on it, he had decided after all not to hold her responsible for Aunt Gussie's blatant matchmaking. Perhaps his changed attitude was his way of holding out the olive branch, his way of admitting *he*'d jumped to conclusions too readily, just as Aunt Gussie had. Whatever his motive, he had succeeded in making her tinglingly aware of him even when she wasn't looking at him.

Stealing a sideways glance at his recumbent form she saw to her relief he was still sleeping. On impulse, she shifted carefully in her seat and, under cover of the magazine she was pretending to read, studied his sleeping face.

In repose and without the impact of those startlingly blue eyes that caused so much female fluttering, it had a softer look, almost vulnerable with the way the dark lashes swept against his cheeks, and with the muscles of that implacable jaw relaxed. He had taken off his jacket and his pale grey shirt was taut across his powerful shoulders and broad chest, allowing a glimpse of dark, curling hair where the buttons strained apart. Unconsciously running her tongue over her lips, Kirsten let her gaze travel up to his mouth, the top lip finely shaped and firm, the lower fuller, hinting at a sensuousness that made her skin prickle in a not entirely unpleasant way. He was certainly an attractive man, she acknowledged, and found herself hoping there *would* be an opportunity to wear that revealing gold bikini.

'Do I have a smut on my nose or something?' Benet asked without even a flicker of his closed eyelids and Kirsten jumped as if she'd been stung.

'I—I don't know what you mean,' she muttered, and buried her burning face in the magazine she was holding. What was it, she wondered. Some kind of extra-sensory perception? And if he could tell she was looking at him even with his eyes closed, suppose he could read her thoughts! She felt his seat return to the upright position and then the magazine was taken out of her hands and returned to her the right way up.

The plane had landed, Benet had guided her through the airport formalities, collected their luggage and ushered her into a waiting taxi, and still Kirsten was too embarrassed to look at him. It wasn't until the taxi had carried them over a long causeway joining St George's Island to the largest island in the Bermudas group that she began to lose her constraint. It was the first time in her life she had seen such exotic vegetation growing wild and her green eyes widened in wondering appreciation. Graceful palm trees and vivid green cacti, oleander, hibiscus and bougainvillaea bordered the narrow, winding road they were travelling along at little more than a snail's pace, sometimes growing so luxuriantly that they met overhead to form a shady tunnel.

Still at the same slow pace they passed through quaint villages of pastel-washed houses—blue, green, yellow, apricot, bright pink and pumpkin orange—and hardly ever out of sight of the impossibly turquoise blue sea, flecked with white sails and dotted with jewel-like islands. It would disappear on one side only to reappear on the other or right in front of them. Kirsten was entranced.

'It's my turn to watch your face now,' Benet teased gently. 'And I don't have to ask if you're impressed.'

Even this reminder of her earlier embarrassment couldn't spoil her pleasure. 'Impressed!' she echoed. 'Oh Benet, I never dreamed anywhere could be so lovely.' She was completely unaware of her own vivid appeal, or of the appreciative smile her wide-eyed excitement brought to her companion's lips.

'Look! Oh look at that gorgeous beach . . . actually fringed with palm trees!' It was on the tip of her tongue to ask if they could stop, and then she remembered this wasn't a pleasure trip. Her face lost a little of its animation. 'It—it's very kind of the driver to drive so slowly so I can see everything,' she said in a more subdued voice.

Benet laughed. 'It's more than his job's worth to go any faster. There's a very strict speed limit here, twenty miles an hour on the open road and fifteen in town.'

'Oh.' Kirsten subsided in her seat feeling very foolish at having assumed it was especially for her benefit.

'There'll be plenty of time for you to explore later,' Benet said as if he had been reading her thoughts.

Startled, Kirsten looked up at him. 'There will?'

'Of course. It may take a day or two before Gene Deland can get here. You're not in any hurry to get back to

England, are you?' One dark eyebrow was raised interrogatively.

'I—I suppose not,' she stuttered. Poppy had been running their little antique shop almost single-handed since Kirsten had been working at the Saker Galleries and Davina Coyle could hardly object to her prolonged absence when it was at their boss's instigation. And anyway, she wasn't sure she still had a job to go back to. The reminder of how Benet Saker had shaken her life out of kilter brought back her resentment.

'No, I don't mind staying on a few extra days, but how about you?' she couldn't resist jibing. 'Aren't you afraid I'll get the wrong idea and see it as encouragement for my designs on you?'

'Oh, I think I'm safe enough.' He leaned back in his corner with such a complacent grin on his face that Kirsten itched to wipe it off. 'Haven't you assured me that I'm the last man on earth you could ever fancy?'

Before Kirsten could think of a sharp enough retort the taxi was turning into a wide gateway and crunching round a well-kept gravel sweep to stop in front of the most charming house she had ever seen. Spacious, but not large enough to be intimidating, the pale apricot walls and scintillating white roof put her in mind of a giant birthday cake displayed against a setting of palm trees, flowering shrubs, clipped grass and blue, blue sky. A fretted balcony encircled the house at first-floor level giving shade to the ground-floor rooms while shutters hinged at the top and held open on struts shaded the upper floor windows.

As the car stopped a grizzled figure, skin the colour of a pickled walnut and almost as wrinkled, his teeth flashing whitely in a beaming smile of welcome, emerged from the wide open front door.

'Mr Benet, sir! Man, but it's good to see you again!' He grasped Benet's hand in both of his and pumped his arm with energetic enthusiasm.

'Joe, you old son-of-a-gun! Still as spry as a two-year-old, I see.' Benet greeted him with obvious affection. 'How's my father keeping?'

'Pretty fine, sir, pretty fine. Has his good days and his bad days, but on the whole, pretty fine.'

Benet nodded his satisfaction and turned to draw Kirsten forward. 'Kirsten, I'd like you to meet Joe Murson. He's the boss man around here and keeps us all in order. Joe, this is Miss Kirsten Douglas.'

'I'm very pleased to meet you, Mr Murson,' Kirsten said, shaking his hand while he chortled his appreciation of Benet's remarks.

'Likewise, Miss Kirsten, and I'd take it kindly if you'd call me Joe. My Bella won't know who you's talking about if you call me Mr Murson.'

'Thank you, Joe, I'd be glad to.' Kirsten found herself grinning in response to his ebullient friendliness. Then Benet was taking her arm and, while two grinning boys pounced on their luggage, Joe ushered them into a cool, shady hall where the polished cedar-wood floor gleamed even in the dimness and where the wide arms of an impressive staircase directly opposite the entrance seemed to offer a welcome.

From the rear regions to one side of the staircase a motherly figure appeared clad in a bright red print dress that strained at every seam, her greying hair confined beneath a matching bandana.

'Bella! You haven't changed a bit. You're still as ravishingly beautiful as ever.' Benet stepped forward to greet her and all but disappeared as two enormous arms enfolded him and a bubbling chuckle rose from that vast chest.

'And you's still as impudent as ever with your tongue drippin' honey,' she rebuked when at last she released him, but Kirsten could see she was delighted with his teasing.

There were more introductions and, though Bella's welcome was as warm as Joe's had been, Kirsten was aware of the speculation in her shrewd brown eyes that slid from Kirsten to Benet and back again. She realised Benet had seen it, too, for there was a sudden touch of frost to his smile.

'What a lovely old house this is, Mr Saker,' she said to put an end to that speculation, carefully keeping her voice cool and polite.

'Thank you, Miss Douglas,' he replied with equal formality, though she couldn't tell if it was a genuine following of her lead or designed to cut her down to size. She rather suspected it was the latter because she was sure she detected a mocking gleam in those disturbingly blue eyes before he was again taking her arm and leading her across the hall and into a large, high-ceilinged room, obviously a sitting room, the floor the same burnished cedar wood as the hall, but in here scattered with rugs in jewel colours, the chairs and sofas deeply comfortable-looking. Cool and shady like the hall, the room immediately drew Kirsten's eyes to the panoramic window at the far end where the luxuriant garden sloped away to reveal tantalising glimpses of sparkling sea and sand, so white under the strong sun it was almost dazzling.

It took several moments for her eyes to adjust to the shadows of the room after that brightness and before she realised the room was occupied. She almost gasped aloud for there, sitting in a wing chair within sight of that wonderful view, was Benet as he might look in another thirty years, the once black hair still thick, but almost completely white; the same lean, clever face and determined chin, but lined with age and pain; the same tall, powerful frame, but stooped and stiff; everything except Benet's remarkable blue eyes: his father's were grey.

He struggled painfully out of his chair, brushing aside

Benet's hurried, 'Don't get up, Father,' his face alight with pleasure.

'Oh, it does me good to keep moving. And it does me even more good to see you, son.'

Benet hugged him, but gently, aware of the pain even a loving greeting could cause.

'And you're Gussie Douglas's niece.' He held out his poor, twisted arthritic hands and Kirsten took them carefully, compassion bringing a painful lump to her throat. 'My goodness, but you've changed since I saw you last!'

Kirsten smiled. 'I know we *must* have met before, but I'm afraid I don't remember.'

'No, I don't suppose you do,' Theo Saker said gently. 'You were very young and you were going through a very bad time. And after that one occasion you were away at school every time I visited Lake House. Which was a pity, because I would have enjoyed seeing you grow up. Not that I have any fault to find with the finished product,' he added gallantly.

'She likes to be told she's not a bit like her aunt.' Benet's mischievous dig made her stiffen defensively.

'Neither is she, though Gussie was once a handsome young woman, too, you know.' In spite of the pain he must be suffering his eyes were full of humour. 'Mind you, even then she did have a tendency to believe she always knew what was best for one.'

Kirsten found it hard not to smile at this graceful way of describing her aunt's habit of riding rough-shod over any opposition, and she was reminded of Mrs Pattinson's hints that there had been a time when her aunt had hoped to marry Theo Saker. She wondered now if he was hinting at the reason why nothing had come of it, and she wondered, too, what had become of Theo's first wife, Benet's mother.

But the question went out of her head as Mr Saker went

on, 'Now that was unkind of me. Gussie has always been a loyal friend and for her sake, and because I'm at last to have the pleasure of getting to know you, I say welcome to Everleigh, Kirsten. I hope you will treat my home as your own and that you'll be very happy here.'

Again Kirsten had to struggle against the lump in the throat at the warmth of his welcome. 'Th-thank you, Mr Saker. I'm sure I shall.' And for some reason she was suddenly acutely aware of Benet's enigmatic gaze fixed on her face.

'Now, my dear, I know it's still early evening here,' his father went on, 'but back home it must be about your bedtime, so I suggest Bella shows you to your room and serves you a light supper on a tray. A good night's sleep is all a young thing like you needs to get her personal time-clock ticking smoothly again.' He bent to kiss her forehead. 'Goodnight, Kirsten, sleep well.'

Kirsten responded to his affectionate thoughtfulness like a flower responding to the sun. 'It's wonderful to be made to feel so welcome when I'm a stranger to you, really,' she said huskily, then on impulse reached up and kissed his cheek. 'Goodnight, Mr Saker. Goodnight, Benet.'

'Don't I rate the same goodnight kiss, Kirsten?'

Kirsten's startled glance flew to his face, and in spite of recognising the wicked mockery in his voice, her imagination suddenly slipped its leash as she found herself wondering what kissing Benet would be like. And then realising where her thoughts were leading her she coloured violently.

It was Bella who came to her rescue, answering Mr Saker's summons to show her to her room, and Kirsten followed her with relief.

CHAPTER FOUR

FOR a woman of her bulk, Bella was surprisingly light on her feet, but she still had little breath for conversation as she led the way upstairs and along the right-hand gallery before pausing to open a door. Once inside the room she flopped down on to a chair just inside the door, fanning herself with her hand.

'Joe's already brought up your bags, Miss Kirsten, and I can unpack for you if'n you like.'

'Oh, there's no need for you to go to so much trouble,' Kirsten protested. 'Thanks very much, but I can manage to do that for myself.' She was looking admiringly round the large bedroom. 'I can see there'll be little else I can do in a house as well run as this.'

Up here, too, the same gleaming cedar-wood floors, though the scattered rugs in this very feminine room were rose-pink to match the silk hangings of a four-poster bed that surely had to be an antique, judging from the patina of the delicately carved wooden posts. Similar hangings fluttered at the two large windows, one that overlooked the gardens at the side of the house and from which Kirsten could see the sparkling white roofs of other villas dotted among the trees along the shoreline, and the other overlooking the sea itself and its myriad small islands, and both windows opening on to the balcony that encircled the house. A silver bowl of exotic deep red flowers stood on the slender-legged dressing table and were reflected in the dainty swing mirror, and on either side of the bed were shelves well stocked with books. A low table and two comfortable chairs had been set in front of one window and floor-to-ceiling wardrobes had been built to cover one wall entirely. At least, that was what Kirsten thought until Bella struggled up out of her chair, having caught her breath, and opened two of the doors in the centre to reveal a rose-pink tiled bathroom, lavishly provided with rose-pink fluffy towels.

She was almost stunned by such opulence. 'You don't look after a house this size all on your own, do you, Bella?' she asked incredulously and the housekeeper's delighted chuckled rumbled out of her deep chest.

'Bless you, no, Miss Kirsten. I has three girls to help out. Mind, I has to chase 'em round a bit sometimes, else they don't do things right. Now maybe you'd like to take a bath, Miss Kirsten. Wash all them travel stains off'n you. I'll be up in a whiles with your supper.'

As soon as Bella had gone Kirsten unlocked her suit-cases, the large, lightweight one her aunt had pressed upon her and her own shabby smaller one containing her toilet things and, taking out what she needed, she thank-fully stripped off her clothes and gave a moan of sheer pleasure as she sank her hot, sticky body under the scented bubbles.

Luxury like this I could get to like, she thought wryly, comparing all this with the unheated and strictly utilita-rian bathroom back at the flat. It was the danger of falling asleep and drowning that eventually brought her out to wrap herself in one of the big towels before dusting herself liberally with a very expensively scented talc and slipping on the wispy voile nightdress and matching wrapper. Returning to the bedroom she had intended to tidy up her discarded clothes, but the view from the window caught her eye and made her forget everything else. Darkness had fallen while she had been soaking in the bath and, instead of sparkling sunlight, now there were hundreds of lights against a midnight blue background so that it was almost impossible to tell where the stars ended and where the man-made, earthbound lights began.

Drawn out on to the balcony she watched spellbound as a large luxury liner, ablaze with lights, seemed to float in the satin darkness. She tried and failed to identify the sweet fragrance on the night air, cool now but not unpleasantly so.

She heard the click of her bedroom door opening behind her, but was still reluctant to move. 'I'm out here, Bella,' she called. 'I'll be with you in a moment, but it's so beautiful . . .'

One of the pink-shaded lamps was switched on inside the room stealing the light from the stars, and with a sigh Kirsten turned, then froze with shock. It wasn't Bella but Benet who was lowering the tray on to the table just inside the window.

'I thought I'd save Bella's legs.' He straightened up, his face in shadow because the light was behind him, but Kirsten could feel his eyes moving slowly over her until she was burningly aware that her only covering was the flimsy wrapper and the even flimsier nightdress. Her instinct was to retreat again to the comparative darkness of the balcony, and she did indeed take a step backwards.

'Are you trying to get a chill? You will, you know, if you've only just come out of the bath. I've come to feed you, not to eat you, so come in here and get your supper.'

She still couldn't see his expression, but his voice betrayed his amusement at her outraged modesty and it stung. She remembered her vow to make him eat his words and lust after her a little, and stepped into the room with what she hoped was sophisticated nonchalance to sit in one of the easy chairs.

'Thank you,' she said coolly, glad now of the glamorous nightwear her aunt had insisted on providing her with instead of the no-nonsense cotton pyjamas she usually wore to bed, but wishing her face wasn't devoid of make-up and that her hair wasn't rioting so untidily after the steamy atmosphere of the bathroom.

Trying desperately not to betray her self-consciousness and wishing fervently that he would leave her now that he had delivered the tray, she lifted the cover from one of the dishes and sniffed appreciatively at the fluffy omelette beneath, spread the linen napkin on her lap and began to eat.

But Benet didn't seem in any hurry to go. Picking up a full wine glass beaded with condensation on the outside he held it out to her and she was obliged to take it, feeling a distinct frisson of awareness as her fingers touched his.

Nervously, she took a sip then returned the glass to the table, afraid the trembling of her hand would give away the disturbed state of her nerves. It was only because she had never entertained a man in her bedroom before in a state of undress, she told herself, and then lowered her head over her plate to hide the flood of colour that unwary thought brought to her cheeks.

'You know, you're an enigma, Kirsten,' Benet said, and she was so astonished she looked up at him.

'Me?' She gave a splutter of disbelieving laughter. 'Have you been at the wine? Plain and ordinary, that's me, or, as my aunt says, a small-town nobody, too naïve for her own good. A girl with *less* mystery must be hard to find.'

'I'm sure your aunt never said that about you.' He had been leaning forward watching her, his hands resting on the back of the other easy chair, but now he straightened up stiffly.

'No?' Remembering her aunt's contemptuous tone as she had said those very words, Kirsten raised an ironic eyebrow.

'And anyway, I didn't mean you were enigmatic in a sexy way. Though you're that too,' he added slowly after a brief pause. 'If your temper's anything to go by there's a lot of passion boiling under that prim, touch-me-not exterior.'

Prim! Here she was congratulating herself on her sophistication, sitting here entertaining him in her bedroom wearing next to nothing and all he saw was a prim little miss! Seething with chagrin as she was, she couldn't help dropping a revealingly self-conscious glance to check how much of her rounded bosom she was showing.

'If having more discrimination than to hop into bed with every boy-friend who asks me out makes me prim, then I'm not ashamed of it,' she retorted in a strangled voice, and he laughed. He actually laughed at her!

'Perhaps prim is the wrong word. Innocent, maybe? Unaffected certainly. And that's part of the other contradiction I was referring to. I've seen you with your friend Poppy. There's genuine warmth and affection between you, and I saw that same spontaneous warmth when you were with my father. And yet with your aunt—you're quite different. It's as if you turn off with her, as if you hide your real self behind a barrier. And I can't help wondering why.'

Kirsten shifted uneasily in her chair. He was too observant for comfort, and he was obviously waiting for some kind of answer.

'Perhaps because my aunt has never wanted warmth and affection from me,' she replied in a low voice.

'Oh, come on.' He was openly disbelieving. 'You're talking to someone who's known her all his life, remember. Gussie Douglas is a very warm-hearted woman in spite of her tendency to be domineering.'

Kirsten thought bleakly of that dreadful time in her life when she had been struggling with the shock of losing her parents when, as a bereft and grieving twelve-year-old, she had needed so desperately the love and reassurance that had never been forthcoming, of how for years she had hoped and striven for some small demonstration of affection from her aunt.

'Perhaps she is with you,' she said quietly. 'But then she never had you thrust upon her as a duty.'

'A duty! Is that how you think she sees you?' He made no attempt to hide his incredulity. 'She's got this match-making bee in her bonnet out of a sense of *duty* towards you? I'm sorry, Kirsten, but I can't swallow that. Misplaced her hopes for us may be, but they can only spring from a concern for your well-being.'

Kirsten didn't quite know how they had got into this argument, but she wished fervently it hadn't happened. She thought of telling him the truth, that her aunt's financial position was prompting her to coerce her niece into marrying for money, but the whole idea was so distasteful she couldn't bring herself to speak of it. She doubted if he would believe it anyway. He had already made up his mind she was ungrateful and uncaring as far as her aunt was concerned.

She put her plate aside, her appetite suddenly gone, and looked up at him towering so accusingly over her, unaware that the memory of past heartache was clouding her eyes and that the trembling of her mouth gave her a touching vulnerability.

'I can't explain my aunt's motives. I only know that's how she *does* regard me. She's never tried to pretend otherwise.'

His baffled eyes searched her face. 'You really do believe that, don't you?' He turned away, running a hand impatiently through his dark hair. 'It's as if we're talking about two different women.'

Kirsten sighed. 'Maybe we are.' Suddenly she felt drained. Pushing herself up tiredly out of her chair, she said, 'Now if you don't mind, Benet, I'd like to get to bed.'

She just stood there, waiting for him to go, but when he did move it was not to the door but back towards her. 'However your aunt regards you, and however you see yourself, you're certainly not plain and ordinary.'

Before she realised what he intended and before she could draw back, his hands were gripping her shoulders and his mouth was gently brushing over her own. She was too startled to move, and by the time her scattered wits had thought of resisting that sensuous pressure, he had let her go and was walking to the door. 'Goodnight, Kirsten.'

The door closed behind him and still she hadn't moved. It was as if she could still feel the imprint of his hands on her skin through the flimsy covering of her wrapper, still feel the strange, curling sensation in her stomach the touch of his lips had engendered.

She shook herself dazedly and walked into the bathroom to brush her teeth. Really, she castigated herself, to stand there like a star-struck teenager just because Benet Saker had given her a brotherly kiss! The trouble was, its effect on her had been anything but sisterly.

But that was only because she was so tired after the flight, she told her reflection severely, and because he had taken her by surprise. Taking off her wrapper she fell into bed and her last conscious thought was the memory of Benet saying, 'You're certainly not plain and ordinary . . .'

She was wakened the next morning by the sound of the curtains being drawn back and a cheerful, 'Good morning, Miss Kirsten. Mr Benet says you've slept long enough and would you please eat your breakfast and come down.'

A young girl, her skin the colour of pale milk chocolate, was beaming at her from across the room. Kirsten struggled to sit up, her eyes dazzled by the sunlight. 'Wh-what time is it? I'm sorry, I don't know your name.'

'Tina, Miss. I'm Bella an' Joe's granddaughter, an' it's after ten now.' She moved across to the other window and whisked those curtains back too, and it was then that Kirsten realised she hadn't bothered to close them before she had fallen asleep. She glanced at the table. Only her breakfast tray with its steaming pot of coffee stood on it now. Her supper tray had gone. Someone had come up to remove it and close her curtains while she slept, Benet? The nape of her neck prickled. She hoped not. Somehow she didn't like the idea of his being there while she was unaware of it. It made her feel—vulnerable, somehow.

She thought of asking Tina when the girl came to the bedside to enquire if there was anything else Kirsten wanted, but changed her mind. 'Thanks Tina, but I'm being spoiled already. I'm sure there's nothing else I shall need.'

The girl left and Kirsten jumped out of bed, tempted, as she sipped a reviving cup of coffee, to linger over that enthralling view from her window, but remembering Tina's relayed instruction from Benet and feeling ashamed of having slept so late, she tucked into her breakfast of fresh fruit and crispy rolls with butter and preserves. In such luxurious surroundings it would be only too easy to forget she was *not* here on a pleasure trip. However warm her welcome, she would be wise to remember her visit here was for a definite purpose. She wondered if Theo Saker had examined the drawings yet.

Washing, brushing the tangles out of her coppery hair and outlining her mouth with a pale coral lip-gloss to match the crisp cotton sun-dress she had elected to wear, she wondered what would be expected of her. But when she finally made her way downstairs it was to find the sitting room deserted and, though she popped her head round every door that stood open, there was no one about and no sound except for the occasional rattle of crockery from the kitchen regions where Kirsten didn't like to intrude.

But the front door stood wide open and, drawn by the sunshine, Kirsten strolled outside. She was standing there, her eyes closed, her face raised, just letting the sunlight soak into her skin when a familiar voice said, 'So you've surfaced at last?'

Kirsten whirled in the direction of the voice and stared as Benet appeared from the side of the house wheeling two bicycles. Almost as incongruous was the way he was dressed. Gone was the immaculately tailored light grey suit he had travelled in yesterday. Now he wore Bermuda shorts with exotic flowers rioting over a cream background and a matching short-sleeved shirt he had left unbuttoned, displaying a large area of powerful chest.

Dragging her eyes from the thick fuzz of dark hair that tapered to his flat stomach, she stuttered. 'I—I'm sorry. I don't usually oversleep.'

He came to a halt beside her, smiling with mockery at her discomposure. 'You don't usually fly the Atlantic, either.'

'No, but that's still no excuse—' She stopped and began again, clutching at her dignity and trying to sound businesslike. 'Well I'm here now, and ready for anything you want me to do.'

'Are you now?' One sardonic eyebrow rose. 'Are you in the habit of throwing invitations like that out to men?'

Her cheeks flushed and her eyes sparked with temper. 'Are you in the habit of reading a suggestive intention into every innocent remark?'

He pretended to recoil. 'Touché!' Then he grinned. 'Come down off your high horse, Kirsten. Can I help it if you leave yourself wide open? Okay ... okay,' he said placatingly as another blistering retort hovered on her tongue. 'If you're ready for anything—how about riding a bike? You can, I suppose?'

Kirsten blinked. 'Ride a bike? Well, yes, though I haven't done it for years. But what has that to do with anything?'

'Because that's what we're going to do today,' he told her calmly. 'You wanted to do some sightseeing, and doing it from the saddle of a bicycle is by far the best way.'

A flutter of excitement stirred inside her. It sounded

very appealing, a leisurely exploration with Benet as her guide, even if, in his present teasing mood, she might find it difficult to keep her cool. And yet even as she felt the surprised pleasure spread across her face, she wondered *why* he was in this mood, why he was suddenly so friendly and flirtatious when last night he had been accusing her of—well, callous hard-heartedness towards her aunt.

The glow died. 'But what about the drawings?'

'*What* about the drawings?' he echoed with a different stress.

'Well, that's what I'm here for, isn't it? Not to go gadding about on bike rides.' She was nettled by his derisive expression. 'Well, it was *you* who stressed that this was purely a business trip.'

'That piques you, does it, that I needed to make that point to your aunt?' Before she could answer he sighed exasperatedly, and then went on with visible patience, 'My father takes some time to get mobile in the mornings so the evenings are the best time for him to undertake any business matters. I showed him the drawings last night and he'd prefer a day or two to study them at his leisure and, as I think I told you, Gene Deland can't make it right away from New York. I also told you, if you remember, that there would be ample time for sightseeing. And do you really consider—' laughter crept into his voice '—that I'm dressed as if I intended to spend the day over business?'

Her emotions underwent several rapid changes as he was speaking, anger that he believed her objections sprang from pique, discomfort because she hadn't considered Theo Saker's difficulties coping with his crippling illness and finally a reluctant capitulation to Benet's infectious humour. And, yes, a stirring of admiration, too. She didn't usually care for Bermuda shorts, thinking them a rather ungainly fashion, but on Benet they were undeniably attractive, the thin, colourful cotton ending about six inches above his knee only emphasising the powerful muscles of his thighs.

'Well, hardly,' she conceded, a grin tugging at her mouth. 'I suppose you feel obliged to adopt the national costume while you're here.'

'The shorts? Absolutely *de rigueur*.' He glanced down at his exposed knees. 'Though it's as well the regulations aren't so stringent these days.'

Kirsten looked at him questioningly and he went on to explain, 'Well, the proper length should be two to four inches above the knee and in the nineteen fifties the police actually had the power to measure them and hand out "green tickets" if they were too short. Luckily, they have better things to do with their time now because I never seem to be able to find a pair quite long enough.'

She wasn't sure if he was pulling her leg, but it didn't seem to matter. 'Well, you certainly make me feel over-dressed,' she said ruefully.

His leisurely glance swept over her, from the top of her coppery head that seemed almost to sparkle in the sunlight, lingering over her smooth shoulders exposed by the deeply scooped neckline of the coral dress, moving downwards to take in the snuggly fitting bodice and the full skirt belling to just below her knee, her shapely bare legs, right down to her sandals and then back again to dwell on the rounded fullness of her breasts. 'Oh, I wouldn't say that . . .' His voice was lazily appreciative, bringing a glow to her cheeks. 'As long as it's only a foretaste of what's to come later. You *did* bring a bikini, I hope?'

The glow in her cheeks deepened. 'Well yes, but—'

'Fetch it then,' he commanded, a glint in his eyes. 'And let's have no more buts.' And Kirsten found herself meekly obeying him.

'I think I ought to have a practice run here in the driveway before I venture out on the road,' she said cautiously, after she had stuffed the shiny gold bikini into the saddle-bag along with her towel. She had intended to collect the rather less revealing black bikini, but then in a last-minute surge of bravado had snatched up the gold instead, a decision she was regretting a few minutes later when, after weaving and wobbling almost a complete circuit of the gravel sweep, her rear wheel skidded on the loose surface and she would have received some nasty grazes if Benet hadn't leapt forward to catch her, dragging her clear of the falling bicycle and crushing her, wildly flailing arms and all, against the hard bare wall of his chest.

She could actually feel the rough, curling hairs of his chest against her skin above the low neck of her dress, feel his body heat through the thin material the whole length of her body, smell the clean, crisp scent of the toilet soap he used, and for those few breathless moments that he held her, every nerve end under her skin tingled with awareness of him. Suddenly the idea of parading before him in that scanty bikini made her feel alarmed.

'I thought you said you could ride a bike.' It seemed an age before he released her, and then he still kept his hands on her shoulders.

'I did warn you it was a long time ago.' She tried not to betray how much that intimate contact with him had shaken her.

'How long?'

She shrugged. 'Not since my mother and father died. I don't know what happened to the bike I had, but I never saw it again after I got to Lake House.'

'That long!' He frowned. 'But didn't Gussie ever get you another one? I'd have thought living that far out in the country it would be essential.'

She almost told him how much she would have loved one, but the memory of his condemnation of her lack of warmth towards her aunt last night strangled the words before they were spoken. Oh no, Benet Saker, she thought, you don't trap me like that again.

'There wouldn't have been much point. I was away at boarding school during term time and quite a lot of the holidays I spent staying with school friends.' She deliberately kept her voice light, but she had no control over the wistful expression in her eyes. 'And for the short periods I was actually at Lake House, Aunt Gussie thought horse riding would be a more suitable way for me to get about. Unfortunately—' her natural humour couldn't help breaking out '—horses and I never got on very well. Something lacking in me, I've no doubt, because the farthest I ever got on horseback was round and round the paddock at the riding school on a leading rein. The instructor had to waste so much time picking me up off the ground, you see. I had a fatal tendency to keep listing to port and slipping round under the pony's belly.'

Laughter danced in Benet's eyes. 'You paint an irresistible picture. I wish I could have seen you.'

Kirsten felt warmed by their shared laughter, even if it was at her expense, and then he was serious again. 'I didn't realise you spent so little of your growing-up years at home with your aunt. I suppose that's why I never saw you again after that first time.' The gentle circular movement of his thumbs against her bare shoulders was having a mesmerising effect. 'Didn't she ever object to your spending your holidays with friends instead of with her?'

The spell was broken and she pulled away, bending to pick up the fallen bicycle. 'No,' she said, keeping her voice flat and devoid of all emotion. 'But I don't expect you to believe that.'

She launched herself immediately into another tour of the drive and this time, although she still wobbled a bit, she made the complete circuit then headed for the gate, not looking to see if Benet was following. Reaching the road she had already turned to the left before Benet caught up with her.

'I had intended to go the other way,' he said, 'but I don't suppose it matters. There's always tomorrow.'

Kirsten darted a glance at him, relieved to see he appeared unruffled by her last thrust. So he did intend taking her out again, she thought, and unaccountably her spirits rose.

Anyway, it was too beautiful to harbour resentment. The road wound through sunshine and shade past the entrances to magnificent villas, all with dazzling white roofs. Kirsten still wobbled a bit on the uphill climbs, but Benet helped, grasping the back of her saddle with one hand while his long legs made easy work of the gradients.

'They do say that having learned, you never really forget how to ride a bike,' she panted, pleased with herself at having rediscovered a forgotten skill. 'And they're right. Like swimming too, I suppose.'

'And making love?' His gaze rested on her flushed cheeks and sparkling eyes.

'You'd know more about that than I would,' she retorted sharply. 'Oh, look!' She braked to a halt as they reached the top of a promontory and gazed, enchanted. Spread out on one side was Hamilton Harbour, teeming with boats of all sizes from sailing dinghies to millionaires' yachts, and on the other side countless small islands like green jewels set in the turquoise sea and, in the far distance, the fish-hook shape of the other larger islands in the group. Ferry boats plied busily among the pleasure craft and a white ocean-going liner made its stately way among the smaller fry to the open sea.

It was quite some time before she realised Benet was gazing at *her* rather than at the scene spread out before them, the look in his eyes unreadable, but the smile lifting the corners of his mouth without its usual mocking cynicism. Their eyes locked and held and an odd breathlessness seemed to grip Kirsten's chest so that she was relieved when Benet finally turned away.

'Ready to see more?' he asked casually, wheeling his bicycle back to the track, and Kirsten wondered if she had imagined those few crackling moments.

'This should amuse you.' Some time later Benet stopped again outside the impressive gate to yet another private residence and pointed to a sign.

'Where tramps must not, surely ladies and gentlemen will not trespass,' Kirsten read aloud. 'Oh, what a charming way of saying keep out!'

'Norwood. Named after Bermuda's first surveyor,' Benet explained. 'He acquired the land in the middle sixteen hundreds but it was his granddaughter who built the house fifty years later. It's interesting because the original structure was built in the shape of a cross to ward off evil spirits. There's a maze in the garden too, copied from the one at Hampton Court.'

Kirsten drew the back of her hand across her perspiring forehead.

'Hot?' he asked sympathetically. 'Come on, it's not all that far now to Spanish Point and there's one of the few public beaches on this part of the island near there.'

'Why is it called Spanish Point?' Kirsten asked when at last they stood on the bare, rocky promontory.

'It's where a group from the *Sea Venture* found evidence that the Spaniards had camped here some years before,' Benet informed her, but his explanation still left her frowning.

'*Sea Venture?* What's that?'

'You don't know the history of Bermuda? The *Sea Venture* was the flag ship of a small fleet sailing from Plymouth to Jamestown Settlement in Virginia in 1609 that was shipwrecked on the eastern end of these islands. The passengers and crew spent almost a year here while they built two new boats to take them on to Jamestown.

They do say it was the tales of his shipwreck that inspired Shakespeare to write *The Tempest*.'

'Really?' Kirsten was intrigued. *The Tempest* was one of her favourite Shakespeare plays. She had even played the part of Ariel in a school production. 'It *is* a sort of— enchanted place, isn't it?'

He smiled at the dreamy expression on her face. 'For the survivors of that shipwreck, yes I'm sure it was. For some of the later inhabitants, I very much doubt it.' He nodded towards an island just off the end of the point where they were standing. 'Cobblers Island. That's where they executed recalcitrant slaves and exhibited their bodies as a warning to their fellow slaves.'

Kirsten shuddered. 'Ugh! How horrible. I wish you hadn't told me that.'

Keen blue eyes noticed the shudder and he took her hand. 'I wish I hadn't now. Come on, perhaps a swim will help to banish those dark thoughts.'

Leaving the bicycles in a shady gully he helped her down a rough path to a sheltered cove. 'Here we are. Not the best beach Bermuda has to offer, but it looks as if we've got it to ourselves.'

Benet dropped his towel on to the sand and immediately began to strip off his shorts to reveal a brief pair of white swimming trunks underneath.

'Th—there doesn't seem to be anywhere for me to change,' Kirsten stammered, at last dragging her eyes away from his hard, muscled torso to look around.

'There's nobody to see but me, and I'm not shy,' he teased.

'So I'd noticed.' Embarrassment sharpened her tongue. 'But being *prim*, I value my privacy.'

'No sooner said than done, ma'am.' Picking up the two large towels he whisked one in front of her and one behind, holding the ends together at her neck. 'Your personal, *private* bathing tent, ma'am.'

Feeling the colour rise under his teasing laughter she twisted round. She felt a lot less vulnerable when she didn't have to look into that laughing face, though she was very much aware of his breath against the nape of her neck as she wriggled into her bikini and let her dress fall to the ground.

'Ready?'

She nodded unwillingly and turned to face him just as he let go of the towels. The silence seemed to stretch, almost as if they had both stopped breathing. Her skin seemed to quiver, first hot then cold as his gaze travelled slowly over her figure, and from the expression on his face she guessed the assistant who had sold her the bikini must be right; it *must* make her look pretty good. And after that first self-conscious quiver she drew herself up straight and proud, a tingle of triumph in her blood because his eyes told her he found her attractive. It was what she had wanted, wasn't it? A chance to make him eat his words?

'What are you waiting for?' she said provocatively, then whirled on her heel and ran down the beach to splash into the sea. The excitement of the chase churned inside her as she heard him splashing behind and throwing up her arms she dived into the next lazy wave and began to swim strongly.

But although she was no slouch, very soon he was overtaking her, his arms moving rhythmically and hardly making a ripple, his dark head wet and gleaming like a seal's. Well ahead of her, he began to circle back and then he duck-dived and disappeared from sight. Kirsten turned on her back and floated, watching the spot where she had last seen him, but ages seemed to pass and still he didn't reappear. She was just beginning to feel the first stirrings of anxiety when something grabbed her ankle. She squealed, swallowing a mouthful of water and came up again choking to find Benet laughing at her.

'That'll teach you to provoke me then run away,' he

grinned. 'You don't have enough speed, either running or swimming, to escape your punishment.'

Treading water, Kirsten watched him advance on her and, half in excitement, half in panic, she began to swim away. But she hadn't done a couple of strokes when he caught her ankle again, and then she felt his hand moving along her leg, up over her stomach and then at her breast and suddenly her limbs weren't obeying her any more. Her legs felt heavy as lead and she would have sunk below the surface if her arms hadn't begun to cling round his neck. Her breasts seemed to swell into the cup of his palms, tingling under his touch, the nipples hardening and sending a sweet, languorous sensation rippling along her veins.

'Take a deep breath,' he said, and mindlessly she obeyed, only to have her mouth covered by his in a sensuous, searching kiss. His arms were round her now, crushing her breasts against the hard wall of his chest, moulding her body against his until she could be in no doubt about his desire for her. And as the water closed over their heads and they drifted weightlessly downwards there was no feeling of panic, only an answering desire stirring in her blood, a warmth and sweetness such as she had never experienced before, making her cling to him, delighting in the smoothness of his skin beneath her hands, the whipcord muscles under her exploring fingers.

It wasn't until their heads broke the surface of the water again that Kirsten realised her lungs were almost bursting. She stared at him, panting, her eyes dazed, deeply shaken by the power and depth of feeling he had aroused in her.

For a long moment she thought he was going to kiss her again and her eyes were fixed mesmerically on his mouth. But then he let her go. 'Punishment over—for the time being,' he said mockingly, and began to swim away from her.

A long shudder shook Kirsten's body and she felt as if she had been doused with icy cold water. Was that why he had done it? As a punishment for provoking him? She watched his arms cleaving the water, moving rapidly away from her. And that was all it must have meant to him, or he couldn't have turned off just like that.

And why should he feel the need to punish her, she thought angrily. He'd been deliberately provoking her ever since they'd met, and yet she hadn't felt any over-riding need for revenge. But then she didn't have his male arrogance, did she, she thought scathingly. Well, she'd show him.

Just how she meant to show him she wasn't sure. As she swam back to the beach she refused to think about the way she had reacted to his 'punishment'.

When she got back to where they had left their clothes she noticed Benet had brought along one of the bicycle saddle-bags and peering inside she saw that Bella had packed them a picnic. Benet she could see was still swimming quite a long way out. Well, she was hungry, and after the way he had behaved she didn't see why she should wait on his convenience. Flopping down on to the hot sand she sank her teeth into a succulent cold chicken joint.

'Gannet!' Benet said without rancour when a few minutes later he sank down in the sand beside her.

Kirsten shrugged, tinglingly aware of him, but studiously avoiding looking at him. 'I didn't know how long you meant to stay out there showing off, did I?'

'Was that what I was doing?' His voice had a hard, sardonic ring.

'You needn't worry, I haven't eaten it all.' She pushed the bag across to him and watched his hands, long and supple as he took out a flask, poured some of the contents into a plastic cup and handed it to her. She took it, taking care not to let their fingers touch, and sipped, her eyes rising involuntarily to his face as the liquid slipped coolly and deliciously down her throat.

'What is it?'

'A mixture of fruit juices spiked with the local loquat liqueur,' he answered, pouring one for himself.

Kirsten drained her cup thirstily. 'Nectar. Sheer nectar.'

Shifting her position so that her head was shaded by a rock, she lay back on her towel. If she could pretend to fall asleep then Benet wouldn't expect her to talk to him. After that incident in the sea she couldn't think of anything to say to him anyway, and she really was rather sleepy after all that exercise.

She dreamed she was in the sea again, and Benet was with her. And he was touching her, lightly, tantalisingly, brushing his fingertips over the sensitive skin of her inner arms, over her shoulders and down the cleavage between her breasts, stroking across her midriff and flat stomach and over the swell of her hips, sensitising every nerve in her body until the lapping of the water and the caressing of his fingers merged into a delicious torment. In her dream she reached for him, feeling again the smooth tautness of his shoulders and back, the thickness of his hair as she entwined her fingers in it, pulling his head down for the kiss she so desperately wanted.

It wasn't until she moaned, arching her body against his that she realised this was no dream, but by then she was drowning in the intoxicating sweetness of his kiss, responding helplessly to the sensuous pressure of his mouth, the probing exploration of his tongue. She felt she was floating and yet her limbs were weighted by a warm, insidious languor, while deep inside her a strange new excitement stirred, an urgency that could only be satisfied by an even closer contact.

She could feel his heart beating heavily and when at last his mouth released hers his breathing was harsh and ragged. She gazed up at him through dazed green eyes, still not sure how much had been dream and how much reality.

'Wow! You really are a little surprise package, aren't you, Kirsten? Didn't I say you were holding down a passionate nature?' He grinned. 'Even so, I never expected to uncover quite such a red-hot volcano.'

His mouth was descending again, but Kirsten rolled away, surprising and so evading him. The dream had vanished and this was cold reality. She felt shamed by her uninhibited response, shaken by the ease with which he could arouse feelings she had never experienced before, confused by his capacity to change from lover to cynic in the twinkling of an eye.

Well, she had wanted him to find her attractive, hadn't she? She swallowed convulsively. Yes, but—

'Now what's eating you?' Benet sat cross-legged, his eyes angry, his jaw set. 'Why the sudden cooling off?'

'There's no need to look so hard done by,' she snapped. 'It may bruise your ego a little to have your advances rejected but it won't be fatal. What I find difficult to understand is why you bothered. That's two passes you've made at me already today, and I can't help wondering why, when you made it blisteringly clear before we set out that you didn't envisage the slightest involvement with me. I don't for one moment imagine it's because you've suddenly been overwhelmed by my feminine charms. So why, Benet? What do you hope to get out of it?'

His mouth tightened angrily and he was silent for so long she thought he wasn't going to answer her question, and then lithely he got to his feet and began to pull on his shorts. 'A man finds it hard to resist the kind of challenge you threw out, Kirsten,' he said coldly. 'To be told I didn't appeal to you at all, that I was the last man you could ever fancy . . . I just thought I'd prove you wrong. And I did, didn't I?' He picked up the saddle-bag with the remains of their picnic and walked off.

Kirsten clenched her fists, her nails digging deep into her palms as she struggled to hold down her towering anger. The conceited ape! Almost beside herself with rage she dragged her dress on over her bikini. He had deliberately set out to seduce her—because she was sure now he wouldn't have stopped at a few kisses if she hadn't called a halt—and all to prove to himself that he was irresistible.

So much for her pathetic plan to attract him and then to freeze him off!

The trouble was—and the memory of it made her even more angry and humiliated—her reaction to his experienced lovemaking had been very far from freezing.

CHAPTER FIVE

BELLA was sitting in the small courtyard outside the kitchen when they returned the bicycles to the old coach house that now garaged Mr Saker's elderly Bentley. 'I bet you could use a nice cold drink after gaddin' about on them ol' things,' she said, heaving herself off the bench. 'Joe'll bring it out to you if'n you like to go an' join Theo on the terrace.'

Benet murmured his thanks and Kirsten felt obliged to echo him, though she would much have preferred the privacy of her own room and the chance to restore her equilibrium.

The journey back to the house by another and more direct route had been accomplished almost in silence. At first, Kirsten had been too angry even to attempt polite conversation and had hardly noticed the passing scenery. For quite a while she continued to whip up that anger because it was easier to cope with than the other emotion she was trying not to recognise—a deep sense of hurt.

It was stupid to feel so hurt, she told herself. Benet Saker meant *nothing* to her. And yet the very vehemence with which she tried to convince herself of this was suspect. Even from their first meeting in Davina Coyle's office she had been pricklingly aware of him. But only because she disliked him so much, she argued with herself, and because each time their paths crossed he seemed hell-bent on antagonising her. But her reactions to his kisses, to his touch, had had nothing to do with dislike.

She had been kissed before, she rationalised, and she had quite liked it. But never before had any man's kisses stirred her as Benet's had. Never had any man touched the deep well of her emotions, aroused in her such a storm of feeling, brought her so near to losing her head. Stealing a look at his grim profile she shivered in spite of the hot sun. Why, having discovered these shattering feelings in herself, couldn't it have been with a man who could share them? For Benet had made it all too clear that her response to his expert seduction had left him untouched.

Oh yes, he'd lusted after her all right, but no more than he would have done after any passably attractive woman who'd shown herself so wantonly eager, and only to punish her for daring to claim she didn't find him attractive. The knowledge was deeply shaming.

She lifted her chin with determined dignity. She might have betrayed her physical attraction to him, but she would never betray her sense of rejection. She would never let him know just how much his cynical manipulation of her emotions had hurt her.

And so, for the rest of the way back to the house, she had forced herself to make light comments about the passing scenery as if she hadn't a care in the world. It had been heavy going, though, with Benet still withdrawn and making only terse replies: and now, following him round the house to the terrace, she felt drained and reluctant to spend a moment longer than necessary in his company.

Theo Saker greeted them delightedly and Joe appeared almost at once with a jug of iced fruit juice and a tray of glasses. Answering her host's interested queries about where they had been and what she had seen, Kirsten waited for an opening to excuse herself and go up to her room, but Benet forestalled her, making the excuse that he had some phone calls to make. Biting her lip she watched him walk away.

'What are you looking so guilty for, Kirsten?' Theo Saker recalled her wandering thoughts.

'Because *I* should have been the one to take myself off.

I'm sure you'd rather have Benet's company than mine. There must be an awful lot you have to talk about. Private things,' she added.

'Now what kind of a host would you think me if I agreed with you?' he teased. 'In any case, it isn't true. I'm not so decrepit yet that I prefer the company of another man— be it my own son—to that of a very pretty girl, and anyway, I don't suppose Benet will be long.'

She couldn't help smiling at his gallantry. 'You'll never be decrepit while you can flatter a girl like that.' She would have liked to add that she suspected Benet would dispose of his phone calls a lot quicker and return to the terrace once he realised *she* was no longer there, but she hesitated to involve his father in their dissension.

She had bargained without Theo Saker's quick perception, though. 'Forgive me for mentioning it but I couldn't help noticing a certain strain between the two of you.' His bright grey eyes were questioning: 'Did you not enjoy your day out together?'

'Oh yes, it was lovely. At least it was until—' She faltered, lowering her head to stare down into her glass. 'I—I'm afraid we quarrelled,' she admitted.

She was startled by Theo's chuckle of genuine amusement. 'I won't ask what about. Neither do I have to ask who won. That austere expression on Benet's face tells me he's done or said something he regrets, but is too damned stiff-necked to apologise for.'

Kirsten grimaced, doubting very much that Benet regretted anything, except that he was stuck here with her until their business with Jude's drawings had been concluded. But the reminder of the reason for her presence here in Bermuda gave her the excuse she needed to change the subject.

'Benet told me he'd shown you the Winslow Homer drawings last night,' she said. 'Have you had time to study them yet?'

'Ah yes, a most interesting collection.' Theo accepted her diversion without comment and then added a twist of his own. 'I gather from your aunt's letters she doesn't approve of your venture into antiques, though I'd hazard a guess that she didn't raise any objections when that same business brought you out here.' His voice was heavy with irony and a betraying blush scorched Kirsten's cheeks.

He smiled. 'I'm beginning to see the light. Gussie's been up to her matchmaking! In Benet's hearing?'

Kirsten nodded, not trusting her voice. Did he know, too, her aunt's reason for wanting the match?

'My dear, there's no need to look so embarrassed,' he said gently. 'I'm very well aware of Gussie's hopes.' He shook his head. 'Poor Gussie. She means well even if her interference does complicate the lives of the rest of us— yours most of all. Unfortunately, she doesn't know Benet half as well as she thinks she does, or she'd have realised long ago her dream was doomed to failure.

'Not that I wouldn't like to see her scheme succeed,' he went on quickly. 'Nothing would please me more than to see my son happily married and, now I've met you, I have to say you're just the sort of girl I'd choose for him. But Benet long ago set his face against marriage.' He sighed. 'My fault, I suppose. My own unhappy experience has had far-reaching consequences. Perhaps I *should* have married again . . .'

He was speaking as if expecting Kirsten to be conversant with his family history and she didn't like to tell him she was completely in the dark in case he thought she was prying.

'But I didn't, so it's no use speculating. Kirsten, my dear—' He laid a misshapen hand on her arm in an expression of sympathy. 'You mustn't take Benet's . . . objections to your aunt's scheming personally. His resentment isn't aimed specifically at you. It's just that, with his mother walking out on him when he was so young, he doesn't trust any woman.'

'I—I see.' Kirsten shifted uneasily in her seat, embarrassed by this revelation and wondering if she should make some commiserating remark.

But while she hesitated Theo Saker added wryly, 'Not that I'm making him out to be some kind of monk. Far from it. There's been a succession of decorative young women over the years, most of them, I'm afraid, the type to confirm him in his opinion of the untrustworthiness of women.'

Kirsten closed her eyes momentarily as an unreasoning pain stabbed at her. What had she expected, she jeered at herself. That he'd been born with that devastating seduction technique? No, a man only became that skilled with long practice.

'It's all right, Mr Saker, I haven't taken anything personally,' she assured him. 'I made it quite clear to Benet at the time that I didn't share my aunt's fantasies. Marriage doesn't come into my plans for a long time yet, if ever.'

Even as she said it, the memory of the sweet intoxication of Benet's kisses and caresses intruded, but the fleeting longing—if only things could have been different—was quickly smothered.

'And I hope I've now managed to convince him I don't intend to be one of his succession of women either,' she finished forcefully, only realising after the words were spoken how very revealing they were. She stood up and said in a strangled voice, 'Now if you'll excuse me, I'd like a shower and a rest before dinner.'

She made her escape indoors, unaware of Theo Saker's amused, speculative gaze following her, and it was only as she passed an open door on her way to the stairs and glimpsed the back of Benet's head as he worked at his desk, that she realised the study, with its wide open windows, overlooked the terrace. Her stomach muscles tensed as she wondered how much of their conversation he had overheard.

Showering, washing and drying her hair and an hour's relaxation on the bed did nothing to relieve her tension. She was tempted to plead a headache and avoid having to face Benet across the dinner table. But she knew she had to face him some time, and the longer she put it off the more difficult it would be. Besides, he would know *why* she was skulking up here and she didn't want to give him the satisfaction of knowing how effective his 'punishment' had been. No, she would go down, and she would be every bit as cool and offhand as he.

She deliberately chose the most understated of the dresses her aunt had provided, a calf-length black dress in silk jersey. With the barest minimum of make-up and no jewellery to offset the plainness of the dress she was confident Benet couldn't suspect her of dressing up to dazzle him and—even though she thought the likelihood remote—neither would it tempt him into demonstrating his irresistibility again.

She wasn't to know, as she lifted her chin to walk into the sitting room, that the copper fire of her freshly washed hair was all the colour the dress needed, or that against her creamy skin, just touched to warmth by the day's sun, the simplicity of its lines had a devastating effect. Theo sat in his usual chair by the window and Kirsten walked straight across to him, not allowing herself as much as a glance at Benet.

'Kirsten, my dear! Just looking at you makes an old man feel young again. Come and sit down.' He indicated a chair opposite his across a low table. 'What would you like to drink?'

'Flatterer.' But she smiled at him warmly as she sank into her seat. 'I think I'll be adventurous and try one of your local drinks. What do you recommend?'

'Benet, one of your specials, I think.' Theo looked past her to where his son was standing at the drinks cabinet and Kirsten steeled herself not to follow his gaze.

But when, a few moments later, Benet crossed the room and instead of putting her glass on the table in front of her, held the drink out to her, she was forced to look at him, and in spite of her good resolutions to remain unmoved, her heart began to thump heavily. Dressed in a light blue safari suit and matching cotton shirt which intensified the amazing blue of his eyes and gave a raven sheen to his black hair, he was arrestingly attractive. Even more disturbing was his aura of virility which was almost tangible, a crackling, threatening power that dried her mouth and made her limbs feel weak.

Resisting the urge to moisten her lips she took the glass from him, proud of her steady hand, and sipped the contents. 'Mmm, thank you. That's delicious. What is it?' Forcing herself to a cool deliberation, she looked straight up into his face.

For a moment there seemed to be a strange expression in those vivid blue eyes, an expression she couldn't read, but that seemed to lick over her skin like a caress. And then it was gone and she thought she must have imagined it when he said with bored indifference, 'Pineapple juice, loquat liqueur and bitters, but the proportions are my secret.'

She raised her glass, refusing to be squashed, and taunted sweetly. 'Then if the bottom ever falls out of antiques you could always find a job as a bartender.'

Theo spluttered with laughter. 'That's cut you down to size, my boy. And not for the first time today, I fancy,' he added slyly.

Benet's flicking glance had all the warmth of a glacier and seemed to pin her to her chair. 'Kirsten will hang herself with that tongue of hers if she's not careful.'

His stinging tone seemed to echo in the uncomfortable

silence until Joe's cheerful voice broke in to announce that dinner was served.

Theo levered himself painfully out of his chair, but when Kirsten stepped forward to help him he smilingly demurred: 'Thank you, my dear, but I think you look far too insubstantial to bear the burden of my stiff old bones.'

'Nonsense. When all you need is an arm to steady you? And let's have less of the "old", shall we,' she teased, laughing and fitting her steps to his slow pace she went on, 'Besides, I'm a lot less fragile than I look. You should just see me humping crates in and out of our old van when we take our stuff to the antique markets.'

'All right, I'll go quietly,' Theo submitted. 'I can see there *is* a bit of your aunt in you after all.'

Instantly Kirsten's smile faded and she stopped in her tracks, biting her bottom lips as she glanced at the hovering Joe. 'Oh, I'm so sorry. I'm being presumptuous, aren't I? I expect Joe usually helps you and you'd rather go on as you usually do.'

'And lose my charming companion to my son? Not on your life! I was teasing, my dear.' The glance that raked her face was sharp and yet held compassion as he urged her forward again. 'Benet can enjoy the company of a lovely woman any time he likes, whereas I have to make the most of an opportunity like this.'

His gallantry went a long way to relieving her uncertainty, but as Joe helped to settle him in his chair at the head of the dining table with Kirsten on his right hand, Benet's searching gaze as he took the seat opposite had her lowering her eyes to the bowl of chowder Bella was just placing in front of her.

'It's a strange thing, heredity,' Theo mused as he split open the crisp roll on his side plate. 'Benet, now, takes after me in both looks and temperament.'

'Except for his eyes,' Kirsten broke in, raising her own eyes to his.

'My one useful legacy from my mother,' Benet said sardonically.

'But you, Kirsten,' Theo went on as if there had been no interruption. 'You're a mixture. In looks you're your mother's daughter. She had the same vivid colouring. But in temperament you have your father's gentleness and, I suspect, his tendency to be a dreamer, but in your case it's tempered by your mother's strength of character.'

'You knew my parents?' she asked eagerly. Her own knowledge of her mother and father was based solely on her childhood memories, happy memories deeply treasured, but now she was an adult there were things she would like to know about them, things she had been too young to perceive as a child. She had learned very soon not to ask her aunt, for her answers had always been hurtfully disparaging. But to be able to talk about them now, with someone who had *liked* them . . .

'I knew Frank—your father—almost from birth. He was a lot younger than your aunt, as of course, you know. Gussie must have been about fifteen then and I was a young man myself, so I didn't take a great deal of interest in him. But our families were always close, especially after your grandfather died. Your grandmother was a very helpless sort of lady, you see, and it was Gussie who virtually held the home together.' He smiled. 'She was very capable and strong-minded even as a young girl.'

He paused reflectively. 'I often think nature made a blunder. Gussie ought to have been born a boy. She was always the natural head of the family after her father died, while Frank with his gentle, dreaming disposition . . .' He sighed. 'But given their very different characters, and the fact that Gussie had brought Frank up, I suppose it wasn't too surprising that she expected to be able to order his adult life too. What *was* surprising was that he ever had the courage to marry your mother.'

'Patti—Mrs Pattinson, my aunt's housekeeper, once

told me Aunt Gussie didn't approve of their marriage,' Kirsten ventured.

Theo grimaced. 'Disapproved is putting it mildly. And yet I think it was the best thing Frank ever did. It didn't change his nature, of course, but Celia gave him confidence in himself.'

'I know Aunt Gussie never liked my mother,' Kirsten said in a low voice. 'She often accused me of being stubborn and sly just like her.'

Theo clumsily squeezed her hand as she toyed with her fork. 'Your mother was neither of those things, my dear. She was a very fine lady, but I'm afraid Gussie had a blind spot as far as she was concerned. She'd taken the responsibility of bringing her brother up very seriously and she was deeply attached to him, but she could never bring herself to believe that Celia was the right wife for him, especially as she had her own candidate lined up, a very amenable young woman who wouldn't have encouraged Frank to assert his independence as Celia did.'

'Daddy adored her,' Kirsten said softly. She was back again in that period of her life when it seemed the sun always shone, when she had been one of their charmed circle, lapped about with love and security. 'She made everything such fun. Even when things went wrong she could make a joke of it. Her laughter, that's what I remember most about her, and how it would make Daddy's face light up. They were very happy, and so was I, because I *belonged*.' She sighed, a long fluttering breath of unconscious wistfulness, so immersed in the past she was oblivious to the compassion on Theo Saker's face and his son's suddenly indrawn breath.

'I could never understand why Gussie couldn't *see* how happy they were together,' Theo said.

A line creased Kirsten's brow as she tried to remember what part her aunt had played in their lives while her parents had still been alive. 'Perhaps she didn't know,' she said thoughtfully. 'I only remember meeting her a very few times before I actually went to live with her.'

'Such a tragic little figure you were, white-faced, stricken, numbed with shock. Gussie, too, was hard hit by that terrible accident. And I did hope you would be able to console each other.' Theo was also looking back into the past. 'If only she'd given you both time to get to know each other then. But all too soon she was talking of finding a suitable school. I tried to talk her out of it, to suggest a day school for at least a few months until you'd come to terms with your grief. But well . . . you know Gussie. I doubt if she's capable of putting herself into someone else's position. Perhaps she thought she'd been too soft with your father when she was bringing him up, and that she should be more strict with you. Maybe I should have tried harder to influence her.' He looked searchingly at Kirsten. 'Were you very unhappy, my dear?'

Kirsten's gaze flew at once to Benet across the table, finding him watching the hand that was twirling his wine glass, as if he had withdrawn from this conversation and yet was listening closely. And remembering his reaction to her earlier criticism of her aunt she said stiltedly, 'I have every reason to be grateful to Aunt Gussie. She gave me a good education, looked after my health. I can honestly say I wanted for nothing.'

Theo smiled. 'Your loyalty is commendable, Kirsten, but you forget I've known Gussie all my life. I don't doubt that she gave you the material things you needed, but there would be other needs Gussie would be unaware of: needs like affection? Sympathy, perhaps? Understanding of an adolescent's problems? I rather doubt you ever felt you *belonged* at Lake House.'

Kirsten felt warmed by the depth of his understanding, but she shifted uneasily in her chair, wondering what Benet was making of this conversation, and she was relieved when Bella interrupted to bring in the next course.

When the housekeeper had left the room again, Theo began asking Kirsten about the friends she had made at school, the subjects that had interested her most, and Kirsten was grateful for this less personal turn in the conversation. She noticed, however, that Benet took little part, that he seemed preoccupied. It wasn't until Kirsten was excusing herself to go to bed that he suddenly said:

'Gene Deland hopes to be here the day after tomorrow, Kirsten, so I'm sure you'll be pleased to know we can conclude our business then.'

Kirsten agreed, daunted by the coldness in his voice and his obvious determination to stress that her visit here was to be short and of a purely business nature. But as she climbed the stairs to her room, at least she had to admit that Benet must have had at least one phone call to make that afternoon and hadn't just made an excuse to escape her company.

All the same, the next morning Kirsten was determined to keep out of his way as much as possible. She didn't want him to think she was expecting him to entertain her again, so after eating the light breakfast Tina brought up to her room, she slipped a cotton dress over a bikini, collected a towel and, without meeting anyone, wandered out into the sunny garden and followed a path that looked as if it might lead her to the beach. There was much to distract her along the sandy path—the exotic, colourful flowers she had never seen before—and there were rough places where she needed to tread with care.

But at last she emerged on the pale pink sand and was enchanted to find a quaint thatched beach house which she went to investigate. It was really little more than a thatched roof supported on four poles, though the back was filled in with two small changing cabins and the sides sheltered by luxuriant bushes climbing right up to touch the thatch and even to riot across the roof, leaving only the front open to the breathtaking view of the sea and its scattered islands.

The beach house was furnished with loungers, but Kirsten wanted first to explore the little cove. It was a truly idyllic spot with its backdrop of green trees and bushes and the two points of the cove fringed by leaning palm trees just stirring in the breeze.

But it was the turquoise blue sea that beckoned and, letting her dress drop around her ankles, she ran down the clean sand and through the creaming edge of the gentle waves to plunge into the silken water. She swam lazily for a while, but it wasn't long before she was remembering the previous day's swim and how Benet had been there with her. And the memories that had the power to stir in her that strange excitement soon had her out of the water again to throw herself down on the warm sand.

She didn't *want* to think of Benet and the way he could stir her while remaining uncommitted himself. She didn't want to remember his callous 'punishment'. She tried to think of Poppy, and whether her boy-friend Jeffrey had returned from Brussels yet, but somehow Benet's hard, condemning face seemed to intrude, and restlessly she got up again, running down to the sea, this time to swim really hard, as if to escape from her thoughts.

And when eventually she returned to the beach again to flop down on the sand that was getting hotter, the warmth of the sun and the energy she had expended made her drowsy. She wasn't sure how long she had dozed before some sixth sense warned her she was no longer alone. Opening her eyes she saw a pair of bare feet only inches away.

'So this is where you've got to,' Benet said, and there was something in his voice that had her jack-knifing into a sitting position, uncomfortably aware that this brought her eyes level with his narrow hips clad only in close-fitting red bathing trunks.

'Don't you think it might have been polite to tell someone where you were going before you left the house?' he went on, and she recognised the note in his voice now. It was accusation. 'I've been searching high and low for you.'

Preferring to be less at a disadvantage if he meant to pick another quarrel with her she scrambled to her feet. 'I—I'm sorry, but I didn't see anyone at the house to tell, and it never occurred to me you'd be interested to know. I thought you said it wasn't until tomorrow that Mr Deland's expected.'

'Exactly. So naturally I expected we'd make the most of the chance to spend today together.'

Wide green startled eyes flew to his face, suspecting him of sarcasm, and yet he appeared perfectly serious. 'If that's not the most arrogant assumption you've made yet!' she burst out incredulously. 'And what did you *naturally expect* we'd spend the day doing? Proving once again how irresistible you are?'

His arms snaked out and, before she could retreat, his hands were gripping her shoulders, firmly enough to prevent her escape, but without anger, and his touch was almost soothing as he said, 'Calm down, you little fire cracker. I meant to start the day by making you an apology.'

'You—you did?' Warily, her face was turned up to look at him.

His eyes were fixed like a caress on her mouth and she struggled vainly to stop its trembling. 'I said things in the heat of the moment yesterday that I very much regret,' he said softly, 'and I want you to know I'm sorry. I'll even apologise for wanting to make love to you, if you insist, though I hope you won't, because I can't promise I won't want to do it again, especially if you keep on looking at me like that.'

The slow, circular movement of both his thumbs

against her bare neck was inducing that delicious languor again. Benet's unexpected apology, his softly spoken provocative words where she had expected an angry set-down, made her heart thud against her ribs and her mind reel in confusion.

'L-look at you like what?' she stuttered. 'I—I don't know what you mean.'

He shook his head wonderingly. 'I really believe you don't! I really believe you've no idea what those green eyes of yours can do to a man. I've never met a girl so devoid of the usual female wiles I've come to expect. I really believe, Kirsten, you have no idea what a devastatingly attractive young woman you are.'

Her eyes searched his face, looking for mockery but finding none.

His hands slid across her shoulders and up her slender neck to cup her face. 'Even now you don't believe me, do you?'

She shook her head, knowing she ought to try to break the spell he was casting over her, but quite unable to move. 'No, and I can't imagine why you're going to so much trouble to try to convince me.'

He swore softly. 'Damn Gussie's heavy-handed match-making! If she'd wanted to ensure we suspected each other's motives for the rest of our days she couldn't have had more success. Look Kirsten, couldn't we call a truce? Better still, couldn't we begin again? Forget Aunt Gussie's—and my father's—hopes for us? Forget I ever accused you of having designs on me. I accept that you have no more inclination to slip your head into the marriage noose than I have, but that needn't stop us enjoying each other's company, need it? Neither of us is looking for a permanent commitment, but that doesn't mean we have to ignore this—this attraction between us, does it?'

Kirsten's eyes widened again. Was he admitting that he hadn't been as unmoved as he had appeared yesterday?

'Oh yes, I know you feel it too, Kirsten,' he said, drawing her closer so his breath fluttered against her hair. 'It's like a charge of electricity whenever we touch. So why don't we both just relax and see where it leads, us? Agreed?'

'Agreed,' she said huskily, the tension draining out of her body as she relaxed blissfully against him, her arms curling round his neck as he lifted her face up to his to claim her lips in a long, lingering, exploratory kiss that made the sky wheel dizzily around her.

'And that wasn't to show you how irresistible *I* am,' he teased, 'but to show you how delectable *you* are.'

The expression in his vivid blue eyes just before his mouth came down to claim her own again made the blood surge hotly through her veins. It was such a relief to know the sniping was a thing of the past, to be able to admit to his overwhelming attraction for her and to luxuriate in the knowledge that he found her attractive, too.

It was only later that she began to wonder if following that mutual attraction wasn't going to lead her straight to disaster.

CHAPTER SIX

'GEE, Ben, I really think you got something here,' Gene Deland's accent took on an even stronger transatlantic twang, betraying the fact that even the cool, forceful New Yorker could get excited.

He had arrived just before lunch and had spent the afternoon closeted in the study with Theo Saker, poring over the Winslow Homer drawings while Kirsten and Benet had gone again to the beach, Benet apparently unaffected by the excitement and apprehension that churned inside Kirsten. Now it was time for Kirsten to play her part in the business and she was still nervous. The manager of Sakers New York gallery had put himself out to be charming over lunch, a stocky man with wings of grey hair framing a lived-in face, but his hard, calculating eyes had made her feel uncomfortable.

'You think so?' Still Benet showed no excitement. 'You'd lay your reputation on the line and say they were genuine Winslow Homers?'

Gene held one of the drawings up to the light then gently rubbed at the yellowing and already frayed edge with his finger nail. 'The paper's right—at least a hundred years old, although it has been known for forgers to get hold of paper of the right age. But then looking at the style, the execution, even the artist's idiosyncrasies—I have to say they all spell out Winslow Homer.'

Benet looked questioningly at his father who nodded: 'I've had even longer to study them than Gene, and yes, that's my considered opinion, too.'

'They *look* right, but it's having them pop up out of nowhere that bothers me some,' the American mused. 'No record of them anywhere, no written provenance to support them.'

'That's where Kirsten comes in.' Theo Saker smiled at her encouragingly. 'She made the find. Perhaps you'll tell us their history as you know it, my dear.'

But before she could speak, Gene broke in again: 'And that's another thing that sticks in my craw. It's not like you, Benet, to deal through a third party. You usually check out the vendor yourself. So how come this time you're letting your—' he hesitated fractionally, those hard, knowing eyes flicking to Kirsten and back to Benet again '—*friend* handle it, charming though she is?'

'He had no option,' Kirsten snapped, before Benet could answer, stung by the interpretation Gene Deland had obviously put on their relationship. 'The vendor insisted that I act for him or there was no deal.'

'Why?' the American rapped.

Theo Saker's gentle courtesy in inquiring into her part in the deal had in no way prepared her for this man's abrasiveness, but rather than intimidating her, his rudeness made her angry enough to retort sharply, 'For reasons he felt were well justified. In the first place he's no businessman, though his time is too valuable to waste dickering over money. And in the second place, he's a friend of mine who wants to see my antiques business benefit from the sale.'

'Okay . . . okay,' Gene Deland said placatingly, though his smile didn't reach his eyes. 'So let's hear what you have to tell us about the drawings.'

Kirsten took a deep breath and, carefully keeping Jude Ofield's name out of it as he had insisted, she repeated the history of the drawings as it had been handed down in Jude's family and explained how she had traced the family tree back to the great-great-grandmother in Tynemouth who had given birth to an illegitimate child only a few months after the artist had returned to his homeland. She told, too, how the drawings had been lying carelessly in a pile of junk when they had first been shown to her, and how, reasoning that such carelessness meant the owner felt little sentiment for them as an heirloom, it had been *she* who had suggested he sell them and let them find a home where they would be appreciated.

Throughout, Gene Deland listened intently, his face giving nothing away, but as she finished he gave her a wry smile. 'Your client has a very persuasive advocate.' His grin widened. 'Maybe he *did* know what he was doing after all.' Then, briskly businesslike again, he turned to Benet. 'And you're prepared to take this information on trust?'

'Kirsten is the niece of an old family friend,' Theo Saker got in first, as if that was recommendation enough.

Benet caught and held her eyes across the length of the desk. 'I am prepared to stake my reputation on her integrity,' he said clearly.

Later, Kirsten was to recall those words and realise how meaningless they were, but at that moment they warmed her to a radiant glow.

A quick glance at Gene Deland's face and Kirsten could see his excitement was overcoming his caution. 'If it's good enough for you, then it's good enough for me.' He nodded his satisfaction. 'I recommend that we catalogue them as the work of Winslow Homer, but it's up to you, Ben. You're the boss.'

Benet stood up, exuding calm authority. 'You've a sale of important American artists coming up in New York quite soon, I believe. Would there be time to include the drawings?'

Gene Deland pursed his lips. 'I guess so, and I know the buyers who're likely to be interested. I can contact them personally.'

'How much do you think they'll fetch?' Kirsten couldn't resist asking.

'Gee, honey, that's some question, but at a guess—' He

named a figure that made her gasp. Even allowing for the Saker Galleries' commission as well as her own, it would be quite some time before Jude need worry where his next tube of paint was coming from.

The business concluded, Gene was all affability over dinner that night, even softening up so far as to make several complimentary and even flirtatious remarks to Kirsten, remarks which, she was flattered to notice, didn't go down at all well with Benet. And because she was still warmed by Benet's glowing testimonial of her character she was no longer embarrassed by his definitely proprietorial manner with her; it was almost as if he was warning the older man to keep off the grass. Only the occasional surprised glance from Theo Saker brought a slight tinge of colour to her cheeks. She supposed that after the strained atmosphere between her and Benet, Theo had commented on little over forty-eight hours before, this new accord they shared must seem inconsistent, but she was far too happy to worry about it.

When Gene finally excused himself on the pretext that if he had to be up at crack of dawn to catch his flight back to New York, he needed his sleep, Kirsten let out a long, regretful breath.

Mistaking its cause Benet said, only half jokingly, 'I know Gene has a way with the ladies but he'd certainly be flattered to hear such a heartfelt sigh at his departure!'

Kirsten laughed. 'It's not *his* departure I'm thinking about, but mine. He just reminded me that we've done what we came here to do, so I suppose we'll be leaving tomorrow, too.' She was shaken by just how much she hated the idea, and it wasn't just that she regretted having to say goodbye to Theo, just as she was beginning to get fond of him, or that her own future was still problematical when she didn't know if the job as Davina Coyle's secretary was still hers or whether she should still consider herself dismissed for insolence. It was the knowledge that away from this enchanted island there would be no hope of pursuing any further the attraction that had flared so strongly between her and Benet, indeed little hope that she would ever see him again once she had returned to the depths of the West Country and he to pick up the threads of his life in London.

'Tomorrow? My dear Kirsten, I do hope not!' Theo Saker protested with charming vehemence. 'I was given to understand you meant to stay on for at least another week, if not two.'

Kirsten's mouth rounded to a startled O as her glance flew at once to Benet. He was watching her, the corners of his mouth lifted into a half smile, his eyes lingering over each individual feature of her face in a look of such intimacy she suddenly found it difficult to breathe, as if he could see every quivering nerve end, read all her turbulent emotions.

'Well, aren't we?' he said softly.

The thought came fleetingly that perhaps it would be wiser to go now, before this island, this man, worked any more of their insidious magic on her. But it was impossible to be wise while he was looking at her like that.

'I-if you say so,' she managed huskily. 'You're the boss.'

A flicker of irritation crossed his face. 'I'm not dictating as your boss, I'm asking as your—friend.'

She clasped her hands together in her lap to still a sudden tremor. Friend? This thing that had sprung up between them could hardly be called friendship. And yet what other word could have been going through his mind while he had hesitated? Confusion flushed her cheeks.

'I—yes, of course, I'd love to stay on.' Relieved to break that disturbing eye contact with Benet she turned to his father. 'Thank you, Theo. It's very kind of you to make me so welcome.'

Before she could regain her equilibrium, Benet was standing before her, his hand outstretched to pull her to her feet. 'Now that's settled, I'll see you to your room.'

A strong arm round her waist propelled her up the stairs and drew her against him as they reached her bedroom door. 'I prefer to receive *my* share of your thanks without an audience.'

She was breathless from having taken the stairs almost at a run and also from his overpowering nearness, but an imp of mischief prompted her to say with child-like politeness, 'Of course. Thank you very much, Benet, for asking me.'

'Witch! That wasn't at all what I had in mind and you know it,' he growled, pulling her even closer until the shape of his hard body was impressed on hers.

His kiss was punishing, asserting all his male dominance against her vulnerable softness, like an eagle swooping on its prey, bending her slender neck backwards as his mouth demanded that hers should open to him while his encircling arms ground her body against his, crushing her breasts against the hard wall of his chest. Yet even while he hurt her, something deep inside her thrilled at his aggressive maleness, made her pliant and unresisting, incredulous that he should find something in her to drive him to such a pitch. And when he stopped hurting, when the strong, imprisoning hands softened to caresses, when his punishing mouth gentled to sensuousness, she had to cling to him or her knees would have buckled, helpless to do anything but respond.

'Lord, but I've longed to do that all evening—' he said hoarsely, releasing her lips, but tracing a line of kisses over her eyes, along a sensitive line behind her ear and down her neck that lit fires inside her and made her gasp. By the time his mouth reached her breasts, pushing aside the thin fabric at her cleavage to release the already aroused nipples, she had ceased to think and could only feel with senses clamouring, heightened as they had never been before. Moaning with pleasure as his lips explored the swelling tautness of her breasts, tugging and teasing their rosebud peaks, her fingers curled ecstatically into the thick hair at his nape while her hips moved convulsively against him, her body involuntarily seeking that even greater closeness it instinctively knew was the only way to put her out of this delicious torment.

He groaned as if he, too, was a soul in torment, and for a moment it seemed as if he meant to open her bedroom door, to finish on that big four-poster bed what they had now begun. And while her mind could applaud his restraint, her yearning body could only feel acute disappointment when he did no such thing, putting her from him to say, raggedly, 'Have pity, girl! You can't know what you're doing to me.'

Kirsten gazed at him with stricken eyes and he pulled her back into his arms again, but holding her this time without passion, gentling her, soothing the fever he had aroused in her and her sense of rejection.

'This is all new to you, isn't it?' he said quietly.

'Is it so obvious?' There was a touch of hurt in her voice because she thought he was comparing her responses to those of his more sophisticated women friends and finding her wanting.

'Kirsten . . . Kirsten . . . you mustn't be so defensive.' He rocked her gently like a hurt child. 'I'd like to think no man's ever made you feel like this before because—well, you might find this hard to believe but I've never felt quite like this before either.'

She searched his face for some clue to the truth of this extraordinary statement. She *wanted* to believe it, but sheer common sense made her sceptical. Even if his father hadn't told her of the string of girls he'd amused himself with over the years, she knew they must have existed. So why was he trying to deny it?

'Just because I let myself get carried away, you don't have to say things you don't mean but think I would like to hear,' she said with difficulty.

'And is that what you think I'm doing?'

'I may be naïve, but not naïve enough to kid myself you're as inexperienced as I am,' she retorted, suspecting him of mocking her. 'Of course you must have made love to other women—beautiful women. You're an attractive man, Benet, as I'm sure you're perfectly well aware. You're successful, even well known in your own field, sophisticated—'

'—and rich,' he finished cynically. 'You forgot to mention what an appeal a healthy bank balance has for a woman.'

Kirsten flinched inwardly because it had been money that had been the incentive for her aunt's matchmaking. Silly to feel this shaft of guilt when she'd refused all along to countenance the scheme.

'You really do have a low opinion of women, don't you? And I suppose you must speak from experience or you wouldn't be so cynical, but I still can't believe they were all like that. I can't believe women wouldn't find you attractive even if you didn't have a penny to bless yourself with.'

'A compliment, no less! And I thought it was your mission in life to deflate my ego.'

He was laughing at her. Her chin came up angrily and her green eyes flashed. 'All right, laugh if you must, but please don't insult my intelligence by pretending kissing me was any different from kissing any other woman you've amused yourself with.'

'All right, I won't.' The gleam of amusement died and his voice had as much warmth as a frosty night. 'You're right, of course, there have been plenty of women. Women, I might add, who knew the score. So why should I let a copper-headed brat who twists every word I say get under my skin? Goodnight, Kirsten.' He thrust her away and turned on his heel.

Stunned by his icy anger, by his abrupt departure, she swayed, fumbling blindly for the doorknob. She wouldn't cry. She wouldn't. But she had barely opened the door before the first sob tore at her dry throat. Stumbling into the dark room she tried to close the door behind her, but something got in the way.

'Kirsten—my dearest girl—I'm sorry. I didn't mean to make you cry.' Somehow the door was closed but Benet was on her side of it, and when he snapped on the light there wasn't even the refuge of darkness.

She turned her face away from him, struggling to fight back the shaming tears, but her emotions had run the whole gamut in an incredibly short space of time, leaving her exhausted and confused, powerless to stem the flow, powerless, too, to resist when he pulled her into his arms and cradled her head against his shoulder.

He didn't speak until the paroxysm had spent itself and then he offered his handkerchief.

She mopped her face, deeply ashamed of displaying her weakness. 'I'm sorry, that must have been embarrassing for you. Aunt Gussie's been drilling it into me for years that it's bad taste to resort to tears.' She tried to make her voice light, to turn the whole thing into a joke against herself, but it came out as a pathetic croak after all that raw emotion.

'I'm beginning to think Aunt Gussie says too damn much!' He sounded as if he was grinding his teeth, but Kirsten couldn't bring herself to look at him. 'Now, come over here and sit down.' He urged her towards the easy chairs by the window but she hung back.

'I—I'm all right now.'

'No you're not.' He pushed her firmly into a chair. 'Now don't move.' Hurrying into the bathroom he returned at once with a glass of water which Kirsten sipped gratefully, letting the coolness sooth her dry, raw throat.

'Thank you. I really am all right now,' she said, putting the glass down.

'I'm not leaving until you and I have straightened out a few things, young lady.' He drew up the other chair and sat down so that their knees were almost touching, leaning forward to clasp her hands in a firm grip. She stared at him, inwardly trembling, but the silence stretched out as if he didn't know where to begin.

At last he shook his head. 'Kirsten, I don't know what it is about you—' For a man who was always so sure of himself he seemed strangely uncertain, the blue eyes burning into her as if trying to penetrate her mind as if, by the very intensity of his gaze, he would unravel the skeins of her personality. 'How you can maintain you're no different from other women . . .' The corners of his mouth lifted ruefully. 'For a start, no other woman manages so effortlessly to make me as angry as you do.'

Kirsten flinched and thought bleakly that if that was true, it was also true that no man had ever had the power to hurt her as he had. 'So why, if you dislike me so much, have you suggested I stay on here?' she asked in a choked voice, trying to pull her hands from his clasp.

But he wouldn't let her go. 'There you go again, jumping to conclusions, casting me as the villain.' He seemed to be making a conscious effort to be patient. 'I don't dislike you. Far from it! Kirsten, I'm trying to rationalise what's happening between us, because you can't deny something is. I find it difficult to believe you respond to every man who kisses you the way you respond to me.'

Kirsten silently shook her head, her cheeks burning.

The grip on her hands tightened. 'So in view of this powerful attraction, is it so surprising we strike sparks off each other, that all our reactions to each other are heightened? Especially when it's a situation neither of us expected or welcomes?'

'I—I suppose not.' Feeling hopelessly out of her depth she could no longer meet his gaze, but concentrated instead on his long-fingered hands gripping hers with a gentle strength. It was true. She had been fighting her own reactions and responses as much as she had been fighting Benet himself, lashing out in self-defence because of the impossible position Aunt Gussie had forced her into. Oh, if only Aunt Gussie hadn't interfered, she thought despairingly. And yet would it really have made any difference if her aunt hadn't tried her heavy-handed matchmaking? Kirsten sighed, knowing it wouldn't. Even if Theo Saker hadn't explained his son's deep-seated reasons for rejecting any permanent commitment to a woman, Benet's own attitude had made his feelings about it perfectly clear.

So what did he want of her, she wondered in bewilderment. If the situation was so unacceptable to him, why did he want her to stay on here now their business was done? In order to indulge in a holiday romance? Was he looking for an affair with her, hoping the attraction would burn itself out? And what of her own feelings? Could she go along with that? She supposed most girls wouldn't think twice about it and, if she was honest, if it hadn't been Benet who had drawn back a short time ago, she would no longer be a virgin now. She gave a shuddering sigh. Even now her body yearned for the fulfilment it had been denied.

'Kirsten . . .' His long fingers cupped her chin, raising her face so that she had to look at him. 'I wish I knew what was going on in that head of yours,' he said softly, then he, too, sighed. 'All that great experience you accused me of doesn't seem to be helping me now,' he said ruefully. 'Believe me, inside I'm every bit as bewildered as you look. Yes, I have known quite a few women, more than I care to remember. I'm thirty-four years old, and I was never built to be celibate. But I meant it, Kirsten, when I told you none of them had ever made me feel quite like you do.' He ran a finger across her cheek and traced the outline of her trembling mouth. 'No woman has ever brought out my protective instinct before.'

Her wide eyes were still uncertain, not because she disbelieved him, but because she was unsure of what he was trying to say.

He groaned, releasing her and getting up to pace to the window, running his fingers through his dark hair as if he was under some intolerable strain. 'Hell, girl! When you look at me like that I'm in danger of forgetting all my good resolutions.'

Kirsten bowed her head. Why did he have to sound so accusing? Why was he trying to make out this—this tangle was all her fault? 'I—I don't know what you mean,' she choked helplessly.

'You want me to spell it out?' His voice was harsh. 'I want you, and if you'd been any other woman I'd have had you by now.'

She shuddered, not out of revulsion but in acknow-ledgement that what he said was true, because only a short time ago there had been no thought in her head to stop him. She would have surrendered to him gladly, willingly.

'But for the first time in my life I'm putting someone else's well-being before my own desires.' Benet's voice softened, took on an almost pleading note. 'I don't want you to get hurt, Kirsten. When I suggested we let this attraction between us have its head and follow where it led, I didn't expect it to lead us so far, so fast.'

Her mouth was dry. She kept her eyes fixed on her hands clenched in her lap because if she looked at him she would never be able to get the words out. 'Perhaps we should do what we originally planned, leave here tomor-row like Gene Deland.'

The silence stretched out so long that she knew he was going to agree, and she had to concentrate all her will on not snatching the words back, on not pleading with him to allow her a few more days. She knew it was madness to want so desperately to stay with him.

But when, instead of the terse agreement she was expecting, his reply when it came was a firm and uncompromising, 'No!' she knew a moment of panic. Wouldn't it be wiser, safer, to cut cleanly through this tangled knot of emotions?

He had moved back from the window soundlessly and when he reached out to pull her to her feet she was unresisting. 'No,' he said again. Maybe it was a trick of the light, but his eyes seemed to have darkened. 'I've got this crazy feeling that I'll regret it for the rest of my days if I duck out now.'

He took her face between his two hands, turning it up to his, and she could feel the leashed tension in his body. 'I don't just want that delectable body of yours, Kirsten. I want what goes on behind those mysterious green eyes of yours, too.'

She gazed up at him helplessly, feeling that already he was probing all her most vulnerable emotions, but quite unable to tear her gaze away from the piercing intensity of his. 'You want me to stay?'

'I want you to stay,' he agreed softly, his gentleness dispelling her panic. 'But I want us to cool it, Kirsten. I want us both to have the chance to really get to know each other. I want you in particular to be very sure you know what you're doing before—well, before you let a purely sexual attraction carry you away again.' He dropped a very chaste kiss on top of her head and wished her goodnight.

Was that all it was between them, she wondered as she watched him depart by way of the balcony for his own room—a purely sexual attraction? But if that was so, why was he being so protective? Why hadn't he just taken what he wanted, what she had been so ready to give?

So many questions buzzed around her head that she didn't think there was a chance she would sleep, but it seemed like only moments after climbing into bed that she was wakened by the rattle of the tray with her morning coffee and Tina's cheerful voice saying, 'Mr Benet asks if you'll have breakfast with him on the terrace this morning, Miss Kirsten.'

The first step in their getting to know each other, breakfasting together, she wondered, nodding her acquiescence and asking Tina to tell Benet she would be as quick as she could. With the sun pouring like molten gold through the window, last night's emotion seemed very far away and it was with a sense of tingling anticipation that she threw back the covers and hurried into the bathroom to shower.

This same feeling of anticipation prompted her to take trouble over her appearance, choosing to wear a very feminine cotton sun-dress with dainty sandals on her bare feet. Make-up she kept to a minimum, just a touch of bronze shadow to give depth to her green eyes, a whisk of mascara to lengthen her already long lashes and a slick of lip-gloss to emphasise her generous mouth. A final mist of light, flowery perfume and she was ready.

It was only as she walked out on to the terrace that the anticipation gave way to a strange shyness. Benet was already there, completely at ease in one of the cane chairs, and it was obvious he hadn't long returned from his morning swim as he was still wearing only a brief pair of bathing trunks and an unbuttoned short-sleeved shirt, his hair still glisteningly damp.

He rose at once when he saw her and she found it impossible to keep her eyes off his long, muscular thighs. A flood of sensual heat engulfed her as she remembered how closely he had held her last night.

'Good morning.' He smiled, the intimacy of his look making her certain he knew exactly the effect he was having on her. But he didn't touch her, merely held a chair for her as she subsided into it gratefully. 'Did you sleep well?'

'Yes, I did.'

'You sound surprised. Didn't you expect to?' He had resumed his seat opposite and was pouring her a glass of fruit juice, but the smile in his eyes when he handed it to her held no hint of mockery, only a warm understanding. Without waiting for her to answer he went on, 'I thought you might like to do a bit of sightseeing in Hamilton this morning.'

'That's the capital, isn't it?' Kirsten said eagerly. 'So there'll be a post office there.' And when Benet raised an eyebrow questioningly she went on to explain, 'If I'm staying on here another week or so, I'll have to let Poppy know.'

'You could phone her if you like,' he offered.

'Oh, there's no need for that.' Maybe international phone calls were an everyday occurrence for Benet, but to her it seemed wildly extravagant and an imposition on her host. 'Besides, I'm not sure when I'd catch her at the flat.' She went on to explain about Poppy's boy-friend being home on leave from Brussels. 'So I thought if I could buy an air letter she should get it in a few days.'

Benet acquiesced smilingly and, as soon as they had finished breakfast and he had changed into crisp white drill slacks and a silky knit shirt, Joe drove them into town in the old Bentley at such a stately pace that Kirsten felt like royalty.

'Drop us off at the Perot Post Office, please, Joe,' Benet directed. 'We'll make our own way home when we're ready.'

'This is it?' Kirsten couldn't hide her surprise when Joe had driven away. Anything less like a modern post office was hard to imagine; an elegant, whitewashed eighteenth-century house fronting on to the street, its sash windows

and central door flanked by painted shutters, its three
other sides surrounded by trees.

'I thought you'd be surprised.' Benet looked pleased
with himself. 'William Perot opened it as a post office in
1816 and it's still called after him. It was he who intro-
duced postage stamps to Bermuda, and if you came across
one of *those* today, you'd be looking at a small fortune. The
park at the back—' he jerked his head towards the trees
'—Par-La-Ville Gardens, used to be his garden.'

He ushered her inside and waited patiently while she
chose a postcard to send to her aunt and purchased an
air letter on which she scribbled a hasty message for
Poppy.

'No one else you need write to?' he asked when she had
seen them both safely into the post box. 'You're not
keeping the owner of the drawings abreast of develop-
ments?'

Kirsten glanced at him warily. Had he hoped she
would? Had he hoped he might catch a glimpse of the
name and address she had been instructed to keep from
him? But what good would that do him now? Everything
had been decided. The drawings were already on their
way to New York and, anyway, Jude's name would mean
nothing at all to Benet. She blushed with guilt at her
suspicions.

'There's no point in writing to him until I can tell him
they're actually sold. I mean, that's why he wanted me to
handle the deal, because he didn't want to be bothered
with the details. And anyway,' she finished hurriedly,
turning away to hide her embarrassment, 'if he's busy he
won't even notice if he's had any mail, let alone find time
to read it.'

His fingers gripped her chin, turning her face up to his.
'So why the guilty look?'

Her cheeks burned even brighter. 'I—I don't feel
guilty,' she denied, too ashamed to voice her suspicions of

his motives for mentioning the owner of the drawings.

He released her without further comment and suggested she might like to see Par-La-Ville Gardens while they were there. Kirsten was relieved that the subject had been dropped and was only too happy to comply, only vaguely aware of Benet's thoughtful silence until he said, 'This friend of yours—the man who owns the drawings—you've known him a long time?'

Again the disconcerting colour flooded her face. She couldn't understand why he should have started probing into the ownership of the drawings again at this late stage and she wished he wouldn't. It had been one thing to maintain a discreet silence about Jude's identity back home in England when she had hardly known Benet, but now, now she felt so close to him, so drawn to him, it made her feel terribly uncomfortable to have to keep a secret from him. She wished with all her heart she hadn't given her promise to Jude to keep his name out of the business. But she had, and she couldn't break her word. She couldn't be as frank with Benet as she longed to be.

'Not very long. About a couple of months, I suppose,' she said awkwardly. 'Why do you ask?'

He made an explosive sound and grasped her shoulder to swing her round to face him, his dark brows lowering in a threatening frown. 'Why the hell do you think I ask? Every time I mention him you look as guilty as sin, so what else can I do but believe you have something going with him, a—romantic involvement.'

'With J—' She was so astonished she almost let the name slip. Could Benet actually be jealous? Relief at finding a reason for his probing and a wild, ecstatic happiness had her grinning from ear to ear. 'Oh Benet, you're as bad as Poppy, seeing a romance where none exists. It's nothing like that. I suppose I mother him a bit because he's so helpless, but he's just a friend.' She wanted to add that never for one moment had Jude made her feel the way Benet could with only a glance, but she was too shy, still too uncertain of him.

Perhaps her expression said some of it for her. His frown disappeared as he slid his hands round her waist, pulling her against him, his mouth brushing hers, feather-light but provoking a response that had her heart pounding against her ribs.

'He doesn't make your heart beat like this, then?' he said softly.

Dazedly she shook her head. 'No one's ever made me feel like this before,' she said huskily.

'Good.' The undisguised satisfaction on his face had all the male arrogance she had once so much resented, but now found made her cling to him weakly. 'That's all I wanted to know. And now . . . unless we want to get run in for indecency—' He let her go, but held on to her hand possessively, and they began their exploration of Hamilton.

Kirsten wasn't to know there would come a time when she would bitterly regret keeping her promise to Jude, when she would recall this conversation with devastating clarity, recall Benet's questions and know that her own guilty reaction to them would damn her completely in his eyes.

CHAPTER SEVEN

'POPPY! What on earth's wrong?' They had been about to go into dinner when Joe had announced that a Miss Poppy wanted to speak to Kirsten on the telephone and because she could think of no reason for her friend to call her she immediately feared something awful had happened. 'Is it my aunt?'

'Hey, calm down, Kirsten. What makes you think something's wrong?'

Kirsten took a fresh grip on the receiver that had become slippery in her sweating palm. 'Your phoning me like this, of course. And how did you find the number, anyway?'

'International directory enquiries, of course, how else? And nothing's wrong, you chump. In fact everything's gloriously, gloriously right. Oh Kirsten, I'm so happy I'm dancing on the ceiling. You'll never guess, not in a million years. Jeffrey and I—'

'You're engaged!' Kirsten broke into the euphoric flow excitedly, her apprehension forgotten. Surely nothing less than her dreams coming true could make Poppy quite so incoherent with happiness?

'You're getting warm, but it's even better than that.' Poppy's laughter bubbled over the line. 'We're married, Kirsten! We did it today. Oh I know, love, I ought to have waited till you got back, but time was so short, and when I got your letter saying you were staying on for a while, well . . . Jeffrey had already got the special licence so we just went ahead and did it.'

'Married!' Kirsten sat down abruptly in the chair behind the desk, hardly able to take it in. 'But—but how?'

she stuttered. 'I mean, when I left you weren't at all sure how Jeffrey felt about you.'

'Well, I am now. Apparently all the time he's been in Brussels he's been missing me as painfully as I've missed him. Isn't it just fantastic? He managed to wangle this leave just to come back and ask me to marry him. Oh, Kirsten . . .' Her voice was suddenly husky with emotion. 'Please say you're happy for me.'

'Poppy, of *course* I'm happy for you,' Kirsten said warmly. 'I was just speechless with surprise, that's all. I know how much you love him, and it's wonderful to know things have worked out so perfectly for you.'

'I *knew* you'd say that.' Poppy sounded tearful now. 'And it makes me feel even more selfish, dropping you in it at a moment's notice like this. You see, Jeffrey has to be back in Brussels by the beginning of next week and—'

'And naturally he wants to take you with him,' Kirsten broke in. 'Don't worry, Poppy. We'll work things out.'

'You mean you'll be back soon?' Poppy asked anxiously, and when Kirsten promised to talk to Benet that night she went on in a stricken voice, 'I'm spoiling your holiday too, aren't I? And I haven't even asked you what sort of a time you're having.'

'Fantastic, but I *have* been here nearly three weeks now so it's time I came down to earth.' Kirsten found herself reluctant to talk about what had been happening to her and turning the conversation back to Jeffrey soon had Poppy bubbling with happy excitement again as they discussed her whirlwind romance.

It was only as they were about to hang up that Poppy said, 'Oh, by the way, Kirsten, you were right about your aunt. She really *is* serious about wanting you to marry Benet Saker, isn't she? She came round to the shop yesterday to see if I'd heard from you, and I did what you suggested, told her you had a heavy thing going with Jude Ofield. She nearly had a stroke! Honestly, Kirsten. I really thought for a few moments she was going to collapse with shock. Did I do the right thing? Only I did wonder whether you'd changed your mind about Benet. I mean, you *have* stayed on there with him . . .'

'Oh yes, you did the right thing,' Kirsten said in a curiously flat voice. 'Thanks, Poppy, and I'll be back just as soon as there's a flight.'

She put the phone down but sat staring at it, unmoving. Lucky, lucky Poppy, safely married to the one man in the world she wanted, all the pain and uncertainty of loving someone and not knowing if the feeling was returned behind her.

She hadn't admitted it to Poppy but the truth was she *had* changed her mind about Benet, or rather he had changed it for her. It was more than two weeks now since Gene Deland had taken the drawings back to New York and Benet had asked her to stay on with him in his father's house so that they could get to know each other. Her soft mouth trembled into a grimace. She doubted if a lifetime would be long enough to get to know the complex character that was Benet Saker. But if two weeks wasn't long enough to get to know him, she had discovered that it was more than long enough to fall in love with him, long enough to know he was the one man she would be willing to give up her precious independence for. Long enough, too, to realise he was never going to ask her to make that willing sacrifice.

Two enchanted weeks, the days drifting timelessly, filled with laughter and companionship and some new wonder; exploring Hamilton in a horse-drawn carriage, the bouncing springs throwing them together as he pointed out the sights, or window shopping along Front Street with the large cruise ships berthing at the dock only a stone's throw away, and watching the policeman on point duty standing in his curious 'birdcage'. Gazing with awe at the two-hundred-foot-long tidal pool in the Crystal

Cave, enchanted by the play of coloured lights against the ice-like rock formations, but glad of his reassuring arms around her waist when he told her the water below the bridge they were standing on was eighty feet deep. Laughing together at the happy antics of the dolphins in the Blue Grotto. Taking the ferry across the Sound to Somerset Bridge and marvelling at the smallest draw-bridge in the world, a mere eighteen inches to allow the tall masted yachts to pass between the two islands. Taking a trip in a glass-bottomed boat from Mangrove Bay over the fairytale reefs. Wandering hand in hand along Feather-bed Alley, Barber's Alley and Old Maid's Lane and up the hill to the Unfinished Cathedral in the old capital of St George's.

Romantic evenings like the night they had dined aboard the *Gay Venture*. Kirsten had learned by then to feel grateful to Aunt Gussie for kitting her out so spectacu-larly. The pleated white chiffon dress she had worn that evening clung to her every curve, displaying as much of her golden tan as was just on the right side of decency, and the look on Benet's face as he had handed her into the car made the blood pound in her ears.

An unforgettable evening, in which she was plied with champagne and fed on broiled scampi, pepper steaks flamed at their table and mouth-watering fresh straw-berry mousse while they cruised on a dark velvet sea between mysterious small islands, and dancing later to a calypso band under an unbelievably romantic sky spang-led with stars.

There had been plenty of dark, secluded spots on board and Benet had unerringly found one, tucking her inside his jacket and wrapping his arms protectively round her because the breeze was chilly, murmuring huskily, 'You fit as if you were made to go there.'

It felt like that to Kirsten, too, as she melted against him, lifting her face, but though his kisses stirred her senses, they remained light and teasing, leaving her restlessly unsatisfied and more convinced than ever that for Benet this was no more than a casual holiday romance he didn't wish to become too deeply involved in.

And now even that was over. In another day—two days at the most—she would be saying goodbye to him, perhaps never to see him again. Suddenly the future seemed frighteningly empty and she bowed her head, biting her lip.

She was still sitting like that when Benet came in search of her. 'What's taking you so long? Not bad news, is it?'

She raised her head at once, painting a bright smile on her face. 'Oh no. Surprising, but not bad.' She took a deep breath. 'Poppy got married today.'

'Married!' His eyebrows rose. 'And you didn't know it was on the cards?'

Kirsten shook her head. 'Oh, I knew how she felt about Jeffrey, and I knew he was due home on leave about the time I left, but I'd no idea they were going to tie the knot the minute my back was turned.' She had to treat the whole thing as a joke or she was afraid her envy would show through. 'I'm afraid it means I shall have to get back there as soon as possible, Benet. Jeffrey has to be back at his job in Brussels next week so Poppy and I have a lot of sorting out to do if she's to be free to go with him.'

'So that's why you were looking as if the end of the world had come!'

He sounded as if enlightenment had hit him and, in case he was beginning to suspect how devastated she felt at the prospect of never seeing him again, she said quickly, 'I *am* a bit worried about the business, yes.'

He frowned, looking as if he was about to say something, then changed his mind. Crossing the study to the desk he picked up the phone and dialled the airport, asking for two tickets on the earliest possible flight to London. And he didn't look as if he minded in the least having their holiday cut short, she thought, as she got up to stare bleakly out of the window.

'The day after tomorrow is the best they can do,' he said, putting the phone down.

She turned to thank him and found he was studying her through narrowed eyes. 'What are you going to do, Kirsten—about the business?'

She shrugged. 'I haven't had time to think about it yet. We could let the lease of the shop go and sell up all our stock, dividing the proceeds down the middle. But that'll take time and it'll leave me without a home. So I might try running the business on my own and come to some financial arrangement with Poppy, perhaps paying her off over a period.'

'Quite the little business tycoon.' The corners of his mouth curled into a smile. 'But even budding tycoons have to eat. Come on, dinner's waiting.' He held out his hand imperiously and took hers in a warm clasp.

Her eyes hidden behind dark glasses, Kirsten let her gaze linger over every inch of the tanned, muscular body lying face downward on the sand beside her as if to impress it on her memory forever. Dark head pillowed on the bulging biceps of his folded arms, powerful shoulders tapering to a lean waist and narrow hips, long, strong legs with their fuzz of dark hair. Loving him was a physical ache in her chest and she had to consciously breathe deeper to try to stifle it. Plenty of time after today to nurse her heartache.

At least they had had this last day together, a day she had been determined to savour, a day Benet himself seemed determined to make memorable for her.

She let out her breath on a long sigh and wished she understood him. From the moment she had stepped out on to the terrace that morning for breakfast she was aware of the difference in him. It was as if time had slipped back as she was caught in the burning intensity of his gaze and that vibrant, physical awareness crackled between them stronger than ever.

She had thought, during the past two weeks, that for Benet the attraction had waned, but as the day wore on she began to wonder if perhaps he had only been holding it on a tight rein which he had decided to let go as it was their last day.

This morning they had cycled to the eastern end of the island again because 'you can't leave Bermuda without visiting Tom Moore's Tavern,' Benet said, and that awareness had been in every glance, every accidental touch, causing Kirsten's heart to beat faster in her breast and her breath to catch in her throat.

He told her something of the history of the lovely old house which had once been called Walsingham and had been the home of Samuel Trott, but which had been turned into Tom Moore's Tavern some seventy-five years ago because the Irish poet had stayed there during his visit to Bermuda in the early eighteen hundreds. They had sat under the gnarled old calabash tree Tom Moore had immortalised in verse to drink their Tom Moore Special Punch and had lunched there on delicious seafood.

Afterwards, they had lingered in a quiet corner and Benet had asked her if she was familiar with Tom Moore's poetry.

Kirsten shook her head. 'My father used to read poetry to me, but Aunt Gussie never had any time for it.'

'Oh, I think you'd know some of it. *The Last Rose of Summer*? And what about this one?' He smiled, leaning forward to take her hand and began to sing softly:

'Believe me if all those endearing young charms,
Which I gaze on so fondly today,
Were to change by tomorrow, and fleet in my arms,
Like fairy gifts fading away,
Thou wouldst still be adored, as this moment thou art,

Let they loveliness fade as it will,
And around the dear ruin each wish of my heart,
Would entwine itself verdantly still.'

Colour flamed in her face. Her hand trembled in his and she closed her eyes on the prick of tears. If only he meant it! With an effort she said, 'Yes, of course I know it, but I didn't know it was one of Thomas Moore's.'

Kirsten let the fine sand run through her fingers as she remembered the way he had smiled at her then, before pulling her to her feet and suggesting they come back here to swim. Dear God, it was going to be so hard to forget him! She could only hope that once back in England the business of dissolving her partnership with Poppy would help. But somehow she didn't think it would be that easy, and she shivered.

It was some minutes before she realised the chill didn't only come from her dark thoughts. Beside her Benet stirred and sat up, looking up at the sky.

'Uhuh, it's going to rain.'

'Rain? Here?' She followed his gaze and saw an ominous bank of cloud had already blotted out the sun.

He laughed. 'Yes, even here. It wouldn't be such a green paradise if it didn't, and we rely on it for our fresh water. You're lucky that since you've been here it's always come at night. It never lasts long, though. Come on, we'll shelter in the beach house.'

The rain began in big spattering drops as they stood up, cold on her heated skin but exhilarating, somehow. She lifted her face to it in a spirit of recklessness. 'It's lovely. I don't want to shelter. I'm going to swim in the rain.'

She turned and ran down the beach, the rain needling her skin. Plunging into the sea was like jumping into a warm bath after a cold shower. When she came up it was to find Benet right beside her, laughing. 'You certainly are a girl for surprises!'

For ten minutes they swam and played like porpoises, duck-diving to the bottom then pushing themselves up to leap half out of the water into the stinging rain.

'Oh, that was glorious!' Kirsten panted as, back in the shelter of the beach house, Benet wrapped a big fluffy towel round her.

'You look just like one of those shaggy bronze chrysanthemums after a shower of rain.' He was smiling as he touched her dripping hair and then as his hand fell to her cheek, tracing her jawline, the smile faded. His blue eyes devoured her until she felt she was being drawn into their bottomless depths and she swayed towards him.

Slowly, as if time had slipped into another dimension and everything was happening in slow motion, his hands slid down to her shoulders beneath the enveloping towel and he drew her to him, his mouth possessing hers, warm, firm, moist and infinitely sensual and, like petals unfurling to the sun, her lips parted in response. A sensual warmth licked over her, making her limbs feel heavy and her head light. Obeying an irresistible impulse her hands explored the still damp roughness of his chest, the silky smoothness of his bare, powerful shoulders, and she didn't even notice the towel slip to the ground as her arms reached up to cling round his neck.

His hands moved down her spine arousing fresh sensations, arching her against him until nothing separated their straining bodies but the minuscule scraps of damp material and she was left in no doubt of his desire for her. The small part of her mind that still clung to sanity warned her that now was the time to draw back, while she still could. And when Benet moved her away from him at arm's length she thought he, too, was having second thoughts until she realised his caressing hands had undone the laces of her bikini and now the limp scraps lay at her feet while his eyes devoured her nakedness.

Overwhelmed by a sudden shyness she covered herself with her arms, but he caught her wrists, gently moving her arms to her sides.

'Don't be ashamed. You're very beautiful, Kirsten. So very lovely . . .' With a groan he cupped her breasts in his hands and buried his face against their swelling softness, and the smouldering heat inside her burst into an unquenchable conflagration.

She cried out aloud in delight as his mouth teased the proud, aroused peaks, her nails curling involuntarily into the hard muscles of his back.

'Oh God, Kirsten, I held out against you for two weeks, but I can't take any more. I want you so much . . .' His voice was ragged.

The last vestiges of sanity spiralled out of sight and she could only follow blindly the dictates of her clamouring body. 'I love you so much,' she whispered, her green eyes hazed with hunger. 'Love me, Benet. Oh please love me . . .'

Even the few seconds it took for him to peel off his damp bathing trunks and to drag the mattress from the widest sunbed to the floor was too long. He picked her up and lowered her on to it, and then he was moulding her against the hard length of his body, his legs twined with hers, holding her a willing prisoner.

The sun was already shining again across the Sound but there, in the open-fronted beach house, the rods of rain still made a curtain of privacy as she surrendered to him eagerly, lost to everything but the wild delight his exploring hands and mouth provoked, taking a corresponding delight in touching him, learning how to please him.

A single cry of sweet agony was torn from her as he took her, but his gentleness assuaged the pain and it was quickly forgotten in the earth-shaking feeling of completeness, of fulfilment in his possession, while entirely new and shattering sensations swelled in a crescendo to a final explosion that left her shuddering and gasping with an indescribable pleasure.

Gradually her heartbeats steadied and she succumbed to a delicious lassitude. The depth of emotion Benet had tapped in her still bewildered and amazed her. She had never suspected the volcano of passion that had been sleeping within her. Certainly no man had ever come near to stirring it into life as Benet had done, and something told her no other man ever would. It was as if his possession of her had put his brand on her, enchaining her now and for always.

'Oh, Benet . . .' Wonderingly she ran her hand over the smooth skin of his upper arm, wanting to tell him she was glad he had been the first, wanting to voice these miraculous, incredible new feelings but unable to find the words.

His teasing smile and echoing, 'Oh, Kirsten,' acted like a cold douche and she closed her eyes on the realisation that what for her had been a cataclysmic experience had for him been nothing new, nothing out of the ordinary at all.

Pain twisted inside her at her own naïvety. What else had she expected? Hadn't he freely admitted he had made love to many women without the slightest inclination to spend the rest of his life with them, so why should she be any different? Hadn't his father openly warned her that Benet had set his face against marriage? And hadn't Benet himself told her there was no room in his life for a permanent commitment? True, he had also admitted that she was the first woman in his life to arouse his protective instincts, but he had made no secret of the fact that his protectiveness only went as far as allowing her time to be sure she wanted him to make love to her.

And she *had* wanted it, wanted it blindly, mindlessly, desperately, unheeding of what it was going to do to her. Dear God, if she had loved him before, how much more did she love him now! And yet tomorrow they were flying back to England, tomorrow they would be going their separate ways and she could only look forward to an empty future without him. Tears of desolation squeezed between her closed eyelids as she wondered how she was going to bear it.

'Kirsten? What's wrong? I didn't hurt you, did I?' She felt his finger touch the wetness on her cheeks, heard the concern in his voice.

She shook her head, desperately trying to regain control of herself, too proud to let him know of the illusions he had shattered. 'No . . . no I'm all right. Just a bit emotional, that's all. I'm sorry to be so silly . . .'

'I suppose we're both going to feel a bit silly when we face your aunt,' he said ruefully.

Her lids flew open and startled green eyes stared at him through a mist of tears. 'Wh-what do you mean?'

'When we have to tell her her matchmaking scheme worked, of course. You are going to marry me, aren't you, Kirsten? You're not going to turn me down because of Aunt Gussie?'

'M—marry you!' She couldn't believe she was hearing right, didn't *dare* let herself believe it. 'But—but you said all along—'

'I know what I said.' He cut her off, his voice suddenly harsh. 'Kirsten, I was five years old when my mother walked out on my father. Can you imagine what it was like to know your mother cared so little for you she could abandon you just like that? From a very early age I learnt the unreliability of women.'

Kirsten's heart went out to the bewildered, rejected little boy he must have been. She had known grief and bewilderment herself, but at least her own mother hadn't left her voluntarily, and she wondered how any mother could bring herself to abandon her child.

'I'm sure she couldn't have found it easy,' she said

softly, wanting, even at this late date, only to soften the blow of that rejection for him.

'Oh no, she certainly didn't find it easy.' His voice was heavy with irony as he wilfully misunderstood her. 'Her new husband drank himself to death inside five years and she dragged out the remaining few years of her existence in a back street slum, then unloaded the responsibility for her son by that marriage on to my father when she died. All right, it's all ancient history now, but it taught me to distrust that emotion they call love and to avoid marriage like the plague.'

Kirsten shivered. Such traumatic experiences while he was so young explained his cynicism and made it understandable, but it didn't explain why he had apparently changed his mind about marriage now. 'That emotion they call love,' he had said, so it wasn't because he loved her. The shaft of pain went deep. So why had he asked her to marry him, unless . . .

'Benet—' She dragged the words out of a deep aching wound. 'You mustn't feel you *have* to marry me just because—'

'I've taken your virginity?' he finished for her. The muscles of his jaw tightened and an anger she couldn't understand flared in his blue eyes. Suddenly he rolled over, his leg pinning her to the mattress, his hands tightening round her throat. 'You really think I'd put my head in the noose just to salve my conscience? I could strangle you, girl.'

Her heart thudded heavily and fright was mirrored in her face at the leashed violence she sensed in him. But she retorted bravely, 'Then why *have* you asked me to marry you when it's obvious it's the last thing you really want?'

He groaned, the hard hands round her neck gentling to a caress. 'Kirsten, don't you *know* what you do to me? From the moment you walked into Davina Coyle's office that day you've turned my life upside down. You're so defensive, so ready to twist everything I say and jump to conclusions.' He paused, then went on, 'I told you about my mother to explain the things I said earlier. It was a creed I always expected to live by—take what's offered but don't get involved. But I didn't bargain on meeting a copper-headed firebrand with the courage of a lion. I didn't bargain on her getting under my skin until I couldn't shift her. I didn't know how to handle wanting her so much and yet being afraid of hurting her.'

He gathered her possessively into his arms, rolling over on to his back so she was lying on top of him. 'I *do* have to marry you, Kirsten, because the thought of your marrying anyone else, the very idea of any other man holding you like this fills me with jealous rage. Marrying you is the only way I can think of to make sure you stay with me always, because having heard you talking about your parents, I get the feeling that for you, marriage *is* for always.'

'Oh yes,' she breathed, amazement, humility and a soaring elation churning inside her. He still hadn't said he loved her, but did she need to hear it when what he *had* said revealed such a depth of feeling? They had the rest of their lives for her to teach him to trust in those feelings, to teach him to say those lovely words.

'Yes, Benet, I'll marry you, just as soon as you like.' She raised her head, looking unself-consciously straight into his eyes, glorying in the strength of the lean body beneath hers, in the sensual contact of skin against skin. 'I love you so much. I think I loved you even when I was fighting you—hating you. And I know I'll always love you.'

'Kirsten . . . oh my darling girl! I'll see you never regret it.' Even as he spoke she felt his desire stirring again and her own caught fire and leapt to meet it. The shadow of the beach house had lengthened on the long dried out sand before their sweet, wild passion was finally spent.

'I know someone else besides Aunt Gussie who's going

to be pleased about our news,' Benet said, as they walked back to the house hand in hand. 'My father.'

Remembering an earlier conversation with Theo Saker, Kirsten smiled and wondered how she was going to contain her happiness. She swayed against him. 'Catch me, Benet,' she said breathlessly. 'I'm going to float off into space.'

His arms wound round her in a fierce hug. 'Oh no you don't. You stay right here on the ground with me. Come on, the sooner I have a witness to your promise, the sooner I'll believe you won't disappear like a spirit on a puff of breeze.'

Theo was still on the terrace when they got back to the house and his eyes sharpened as they approached him hand in hand. 'What's this, then? You both look as if you've just discovered the pirate's treasure.'

'Better than that, Dad.' Benet drew her into the circle of his arm. 'Kirsten's just promised to marry me.'

Kirsten was deeply touched by the look of joy on the older man's face as he struggled painfully to his feet to pump Benet's hand and slap his shoulder. 'My boy, that's the best news I've ever heard.' Then Kirsten was enveloped in his welcoming arms. 'Thank you, my dear. Thank you for giving my son the gift of your loving heart.'

A lump rose in her throat at the sincerity of his words, and before she could swallow it Theo was ringing the bell on the table at his side. 'Joe! Some champagne, Joe. And fetch Bella out too to drink with us. We're celebrating Benet's and Kirsten's engagement. They're going to be married.'

Joe's wide grin and Bella's delighted chuckle betrayed their pleasure at the news and Kirsten felt warmed by their good wishes. The talk was so excited that no one heard the car arriving at the front of the house and their first intimation of a visitor was the door chimes.

'Whoever it is, bring them through to join our celebration,' Theo directed when Joe moved off to see who it was.

Kirsten's jaw drapped in stunned amazement a few minutes later when a familiar figure emerged on to the terrace. 'Aunt Gussie!'

'What is it? Extra-sensory perception?'

'Gussie, my dear, how opportune.'

They all spoke at once, but it was Theo who went on, 'I can't imagine what's prompted this most welcome visit of yours but you're the one person we needed to complete the family. Gussie, my dear, you'll be delighted to know you've got your wish at last. These two dear young people are going to get married.'

But Gussie Douglas looked anything but delighted. Her face was flushed and perspiring from the heat, but there was a white line round her grim mouth and her eyes were fixed like gimlets on Kirsten as she snapped, 'Indeed? Then perhaps you'd better explain, Kirsten, how it is that only two days ago your flat-mate was telling me you were deep in the throes of a love affair with Jude Ofield?'

A wave of horrified colour rolled up Kirsten's neck and into her cheeks. How could she possibly have known that the well-meant lie would rebound upon her like this? She felt Benet's arm around her shoulders stiffen in shock.

'It's not true, Benet,' she assured him quickly, her heart turning over at the look of incredulous anguish on his face. 'Oh, I know I did ask Poppy—well, you know how embarrassed I was, we both were, when Aunt Gussie tried to throw us together. I-It seemed a good idea at the time to make her see that there was no possibility of you and me—' She was making a mess of her garbled explanation and made a supreme effort to be more lucid. 'Before I came away I arranged with Poppy to hint to my aunt that I was heavily involved with some boy-friend. It's not true, of course, not a word of it. We just picked on Jude's name at random.'

'But you do know Jude Ofield?' Benet's face was wiped clear of all expression, his arm falling away from her and dropping to his side.

'Yes, but—'

'How well?'

Kirsten looked up at him fearfully. There was nothing of the lover about him now. The happiness of only a few moments ago seemed to be slipping through her fingers and all because of a stupid misunderstanding. 'Look, I know it was silly to have cooked up a story like that, but there's never been anything like that between Jude and me. He—he's just a man I know—a friend.'

'A friend?' He took her up with the speed of a striking snake. 'He wouldn't be the same "friend" who owns the drawings by any chance?'

Kirsten bit her lip. She'd promised Jude not to mention his name but surely, in the circumstances, he couldn't object?

But even as she hesitated, Benet seized her shoulders, shaking her roughly. 'Would it, Kirsten?' His face was pale beneath his tan and as unyielding as carved marble, the strange glitter in his eyes putting fear into her heart. Then before she had the chance to answer he was thrusting her from him. 'You don't have to admit it. Your guilty face tells me I'm right.'

As she staggered to regain her balance she saw an ashen-faced Theo Saker slump heavily into his chair. 'You'd better get on to Gene Deland and have him withdraw the drawings from the sale at once, Benet.'

'Drawings? What drawings?' Aunt Gussie demanded, and as she listened to Benet's terse explanation she visibly sagged. 'I *knew* there had to be something shady going on as soon as I heard Jude Ofield's name, but I never imagined anything like this,' she whispered. Then she rounded on her niece with vindictive fury. 'How *could* you, Kirsten! How could you align yourself with that—that creature against people who are my friends—people who've never done you a moment's harm?'

Kirsten shook her head in bewilderment. She felt as if she had strayed into some mad-hatter's tea party, as if there was some vital part of this crazy jigsaw that was missing. She didn't understand anything of what was going on, except that the man who such a brief time ago had begged her to marry him was now looking at her as if he hated her.

'Will somebody please explain what I'm supposed to have done?' she pleaded, and when no one seemed willing she appealed to the older man. 'Mr Saker, *why* do the drawings have to be withdrawn from sale?'

'Because if they belong to Jude Ofield they are almost certainly fakes,' he said heavily.

'Fakes!' Kirsten was stunned. 'But how could they be? You examined them yourself. And Gene Deland. You were both satisfied they were genuine Winslow Homers.'

He leaned back in his chair looking deathly tired. 'Oh, they're clever fakes, I'll admit, but then no one's ever disputed that Jude's a clever artist.'

'I still don't understand.' Kirsten felt herself the target of three pairs of accusing eyes and drew her beach wrap more closely round her. 'All right, so the drawings do belong to Jude and he *is* an artist. But why should that make them fakes?'

'Oh, come on, Kirsten. The plot's blown so you can stop the innocent act,' Benet said harshly. 'You know as well as I do that the drawings are as fake as that family tree you assured me so convincingly you'd checked.'

'But I *did* check it,' she began to protest when Theo Saker broke in quietly.

'Kirsten, I'm sure there must be an innocent explanation for your connection in all this, but there is no way Jude Ofield could have come by those drawings the way you claim he did, or that the family tree connecting his mother with the artist could be genuine. I knew his mother intimately. She was my former wife. Jude is Benet's half-brother.'

Kirsten sank into the nearest chair as the shock took the strength from her legs. Jude was Benet's half-brother! It was the missing piece of the puzzle, the reason Jude's name had caused such consternation. They weren't a bit alike—except for the remarkable blue eyes they shared. But still she'd never guessed. And why hadn't Jude mentioned the relationship? An appalled horror began to creep up on her. Suppose everything they had said about Jude was true. Suppose he *had* tried to use her to perpetrate an art fraud!

Just suppose Jude *did* have the ability to fake another artist's work so brilliantly; what would be his motive? Money? A strong motive for many men, but Jude? Kirsten had never known anyone less mercenary. Money seemed to have no meaning for him. When he had any, he spent it, when he didn't, he got along just as happily without it. And to have laid such an elaborate plot! She thought of Jude's laughing eyes without a hint of guile and she found it too much to believe. And yet there was the indisputable fact that he had deceived her over the family tree and he had failed to mention his relationship to Benet.

She licked her dry lips and looked up at the man she loved. 'Benet, I had no idea Jude even knew you, let alone that he was your half-brother.'

He laughed in her face, and it wasn't a pleasant laugh. 'You really expect me to believe you've lived at Lake House since you were twelve years old and you've never heard Jude Ofield mentioned?'

She flinched at his disbelief but managed to say levelly, 'You forget I was away at boarding school until I was nineteen and I do assure you I never once heard the Sakers' private affairs discussed in my aunt's house.'

'Not even when he walked into the Mayfair gallery to

slash a priceless picture on show and got six months in gaol for his pains,' he jeered.

Her shocked 'No!' seemed to register for he went on savagely, 'Oh this is by no means the first time Jude's crazy, obsessive jealousy has tried to damage me. And I must say it was a very clever stroke of his to use *you* to dupe me this time—someone with family connections who actually worked for my company, a girl who can put on such an act of honesty and integrity she even had *me* fooled for a while. What inducements did he hold out to persuade you to go along with his plan, Kirsten? A cut of the profits? Or is he such a fantastic lover you were besotted enough to go along with any of his devious schemes?'

'No!' The denial was torn from her in an anguished gasp. 'You can't really think that I knew—'

But he did. She stared at him with stricken eyes. He actually believed she had been a willing partner in the plot to defraud him. After all they had shared this afternoon he could still believe she would do that to him?

'Benet, I didn't know what Jude was trying to do, truly I didn't. I'd *never* have agreed. He fooled me just as surely as he fooled you.'

He made a gesture of repudiation. 'I'm sick of your lies . . .'

'Benet!' Theo Saker's voice broke in sharply. 'Aren't you over-reacting? We all know Jude has a glib tongue so it *is* possible Kirsten was an innocent dupe. Can't you give her the benefit of the doubt?'

Benet turned away to stare out over the garden, his hands clenching and unclenching at his sides. 'No, I can't,' he said at last in a strangled voice. 'I'm remembering the look on her face every single time I brought up the subject of the owner of the drawings—a picture of guilt.' He turned then, an implacable stranger, and said cruelly, 'Whose idea was it, Kirsten, to go to the length of sleeping with me in order to lull my suspicions? Yours or Jude's?

And how did you mean to explain to him our engagement? Or had you already decided to change horses—that I was a better bet than my brother?'

Kirsten shrivelled in her chair like a tender plant in a blast of frost. His accusations were bitterly unjust when he had given her no chance to defend herself, but she could understand that a lot of his anger sprang from hurt if he really believed those accusations were true. What she couldn't forgive was the way he had turned an experience that for her had been a most wonderful and beautiful thing into something sordid and shameful.

Aunt Gussie drew in her breath in a shocked hiss. 'You little . . . Oh, but you're your mother's daughter all right,' she said with loathing. 'Benet, if I'd suspected for a moment what she was capable of, I'd never have suggested—'

'Oh don't worry, Gussie, the engagement no longer stands. The moment we get back to London tomorrow I shall hope never to see your niece again.' His cold, contemptuous glance raked her shivering body still clad only in a bikini and a beach wrap, then he turned on his heel and walked into the house.

CHAPTER EIGHT

Kirsten sat alone in the first-class section of the aircraft. Although there was an empty seat beside her, Benet had chosen to sit elsewhere, and in a way it was a relief. Their flight had been delayed several hours and it had been a devastating experience to spend those hours with a man who was determined to ignore her existence, who seemed to look right through her as if she wasn't there.

Her head ached and her eyes felt gritty after her wakeful night and she longed for the oblivion of sleep to blot out the tearing pain of Benet's rejection, but her mind persisted in reliving that terrible scene on the terrace of Everleigh when her happiness had turned to dust and ashes. She had told the truth but still no one would believe her, her aunt turning away from her in contemptuous disgust, Theo Saker's bent shoulders bowing even more, his eyes haunted; even Joe and Bella withdrawing their goodwill, sending her sidelong, reproachful glances. But it was Benet's disbelief, his unwillingness to listen that had pierced her to the very soul. After their abandoned passion such a short time before, after his joyful possession of her that had bound her to him forever, his callous repudiation of her was more than she could bear and she had spent the rest of her remaining time at Everleigh shut in her room, knowing that in Benet's eyes it would only confirm her guilt but knowing, too, that she didn't have the strength to face his cold contempt over the dinner table.

There had been no sign of her aunt when it had been time for them to leave for the airport and Benet had ignored Kirsten as he helped Joe stow the luggage in the boot of the car, but Theo Saker had come out to say goodbye to her and the regret in his eyes had brought her tears welling up.

'I wish there was some way I could convince you I was telling the truth,' she whispered brokenly. 'I can't bear to have you think I could be party to such a deliberate deception.'

He took her hand, his expression full of compassion. 'I do believe you, my dear.'

'You do?' Her heart lifted but plunged again as she glanced across at the tall figure waiting impatiently by the car. 'But Benet . . .'

Theo sighed. 'Benet's not thinking, he's only feeling just now. He's always been distrustful of women and you're the first one ever to get under that guard. He's reacting like any male animal who's been badly hurt, attacking in self-defence. I can only hope that once he's had time to reflect . . .'

Kirsten thought of his words as the order came to fasten seatbelts and extinguish cigarettes for the descent. Somehow she didn't think any amount of reflection would change Benet's mind about her. Nothing short of tangible proof of her innocence would do that, and the only person who could supply that proof was Jude.

Hope stirred inside her as the lights of London began to prick out of the darkness. Jude could clear her name. If she could persuade Benet to visit his half-brother with her, Jude would surely tell him she was innocent of complicity in the fraud, that she had been unknowingly used. Benet had said Jude was obsessively jealous of him and had tried to hurt him before, and she supposed she had to believe it, but Jude had no reason to be jealous of her, no reason to want her to suffer by his apparent vendetta against his half-brother.

But it seemed even this small hope was doomed to be dashed. When they had landed and collected their lug-

gage, Benet said distantly without once looking at her, 'I'll
find you a taxi to take you to the station.'

For the first time, anger subdued the tearing hurt inside
her. This was the man who only thirty-six hours ago had
wanted to protect her, had declared he couldn't bear to
spend the rest of his life without her, and now not only was
he prepared to abandon her in the middle of London in the
early hours of the morning, but he was so ready to believe
she was a deceitful cheat he was determined to withhold
any chance of being proved wrong.

He had already taken a step away from her when she
said challengingly, 'You're going to let Jude get away with
it, then?'

He stopped, his back rigid, but he didn't turn round.
'He hasn't got away with anything. Thanks to Gussie,
we've uncovered your devious little plot in time.'

'Hasn't he? If, as you claim, Jude's aim was to hurt you
then I think he's succeeded beyond his wildest dreams.
And you're letting him do this to us without making the
slightest effort to stop him.' Her voice shook but she
ploughed on resolutely, knowing she was fighting for her
future happiness. 'There are only two people who know
the truth of all this, me and Jude. You won't believe me,
but Jude can corroborate the fact that I knew nothing of
what he was planning. I'm not afraid to confront him with
you if it's the only way of convincing you of the truth.'

He did turn then, but only to say coldly, 'Jude Ofield is
incapable of recognising the truth.'

Her shoulders sagged; she felt defeated by his implaca-
bility. 'Then that's one thing you two have in common,
because you're not capable of it either,' she said flatly. 'Or
is it that you're afraid of the truth? Perhaps your precious
pride couldn't take having to admit you've misjudged
me?' Admitting the uselessness of further argument she
picked up her suitcase and began to walk towards the taxi
rank.

She hadn't gone many steps before the case was taken out of her grasp. 'All right, we'll confront Jude together,' he conceded, but the granite hardness of his face hadn't yielded an inch.

But for Kirsten it was concession enough. Sitting in the car beside the silent Benet as they drove west she enacted in her imagination scene after scene of their reconciliation and, though the fact that he had doubted her at all still hurt, she was happily confident that in a short time they would be able to forget it had ever happened.

The sun was shining on the empty pavements and bathing the towers of the cathedral in a golden glow as they drove into the town. For the first time Benet broke the silence. 'It's early. I'd better take you to the flat and collect you again later.'

'No.' Kirsten's response was immediate and determined. 'I don't care how early it is, I want to get this settled once and for all.' She directed Benet to the street beyond the park where his half-brother lived and, shrugging, he complied.

The house looked even shabbier than she remembered as she led the way up to the top floor, and her nose wrinkled at the stale cooking smells as she rapped on Jude's door. At an irritable, 'Come in, it's not locked,' she pushed it open.

The red-headed, red-bearded artist, dressed only in paint-stained jeans, and pouring boiling water from a kettle into a mug turned his head and his face split into a grin. 'Long time no see. I was beginning to think you'd vamoosed with the loot. What's happening, then? Have you managed to unload the—' His voice broke off and his grin faded as Benet emerged into the room from the dark passage.

'Oh-oh! We've been rumbled.'

'*You've* been rumbled, Jude,' Kirsten corrected him quickly, because in Benet's present mood that accidental 'we' must have sounded damning. For the first time her confidence in Jude telling the truth and clearing her began to slip. 'So those drawings *were* fakes?'

'Sure they were.' Calmly he picked up a carton of milk and stirred it into his coffee. 'And I would have sworn they were good enough to fool you, Benet.'

'They did—until *your* name was mentioned,' Benet snapped.

Jude shot Kirsten a look of acute dislike. 'I might have known I couldn't trust a woman to keep her lip buttoned.'

'It wasn't Kirsten who gave you away. On the contrary, she kept your secret so well she fooled me completely.' A look of naked pain flickered across Benet's face as he added, 'You might even say she went over and beyond what was necessary to take me in.'

'He thinks we're in this together, Jude. Tell him it isn't true.' In her anxiety Kirsten gripped his arm. 'Tell him the truth—that I had no idea what you were up to. Please, Jude. This is terribly important to me.'

Jude looked at her curiously before glancing at Benet and a grin of unholy glee split his face. 'Don't tell me you fell for my big brother, Kirsten! And he for you? And now naturally he's a bit peeved to think you weren't quite straight with him? What do you want me to tell him, darling? That I managed to scrape acquaintance with you because I knew you were not only a friend of the family but that you actually worked at the gallery, too? That I showed you the drawings and let you think it was *your* idea to sell them through Sakers? That I drew up a fake family tree and let you hare all over the country checking it out? That I preyed on your innocence and used you for my own wicked ends?'

'It's the truth!' she whispered. It was, but the way he was telling it made it sound like a pack of lies.

She recoiled from him but she moved too late. His arm grabbed her round the waist and pulled her to him, ignoring her struggles. 'He wouldn't believe it, you know, but never mind. I'll help you to forget him. You should've known, love, I'd never swallow losing you to *him*.'

'Don't worry, Jude, there's no likelihood of that. You're welcome to her. If ever two conniving cheats were suited to each other, you two are.' Benet's voice was ugly in his bitter anger. 'I don't know what you hoped to gain by insisting on going through this charade, Kirsten. Perhaps an extra twist of the knife in my gut? Well, I hope you're satisfied now, because I've had more than enough.' He turned to go.

'Benet . . .' Her despairing cry followed him, but her only answer was the reverberating slam of the door.

Frantically Kirsten beat her fists against Jude's chest. 'How could you, Jude? How could you do such a cruel, terrible thing?'

He released her so abruptly she staggered. 'I couldn't let a chance like that go by, now could I?' He stirred his coffee slowly, as if relishing the pain he had just inflicted. 'Oh, it would've been very satisfying if the original plan had gone through. I meant to wait until the drawings were sold and then get on to the newspapers, tell the world they were fakes and that knowing it, my upright brother had still gone ahead and put them up for auction. I wouldn't have given much for the reputation of Saker Galleries then, would you? But that would've only clobbered his reputation. This time I've got him where it really hurts—in his manhood. Oh, you handed him to me on a plate, Kirsten. Once I realised he cared for you—it was too, too easy.'

'And what about me?' Tears rolled unheeded down her cheeks. 'Doesn't it matter that you're hurting me too?'

He shrugged dismissively. 'I dare say you'll get over it.'

'Why?' she whispered. 'Why do you hate him so much?'

'You have to ask that?' His face was suddenly ugly with vindictiveness. 'We shared the same mother, but he's never known what it is to be in want. Born into luxury he's had everything—wealth, education, a ready-made business to walk into, and all without having to lift a finger. He even had you! Then look at me, beaten by a drunken father, dragged up in poverty by a widowed mother than an object of charity to the legitimate side of the family after she died. All my worldly goods wouldn't fill a suitcase, and *I'm* the one with the talent,' he finished bitterly.

'Yes, you are, and what are you doing with it? Wasting it. Throwing it away because you get more satisfaction scoring off your brother.' Kirsten felt too sickened by him to even consider the danger of pouring such scorn on a man who had already proved himself slightly unbalanced. 'Who would think to look at you, that inside you could be such a mean-minded, self-pitying weakling!'

'Why you little—' Enraged he advanced on her, his arm raised to strike her.

But Kirsten didn't flinch. Gripped by a despair that was beyond fear she made no effort to defend herself. 'Yes, hit me. Beat me to a pulp. Do you think I care? Do you think there's any way you can hurt me more than you already have?'

His enraged rush faltered, his arm falling to his side. 'Oh . . . get out of here,' he growled, turning away.

Kirsten walked back to the flat, too numbed to think, too numbed even to feel any more. It wasn't until she found her suitcase in the doorway of the still unopened shop where Benet must have dropped it that the feeling began to flow back, an overwhelming feeling of deprivation and loss, because it finally brought home to her that her only chance of proving her innocence had failed and that she would never see the man she loved so desperately again. She was shaking so badly it was some time before she could raise the strength to pick up the suitcase, unlock the door and carry it upstairs.

She had hardly reached the landing when the sitting

room door flew open and Poppy hurtled towards her in an exuberant greeting. 'Kirsten, love, it's so good to see you! We thought you'd be back last night.'

It was funny, but with so much on her mind Kirsten had forgotten Poppy and the fact that her friend was now a married woman. A knife seemed to twist in her breast, but not for anything would she spoil Poppy's obviously delirious happiness by betraying her own misery.

'The flight was delayed,' she managed to explain before Poppy dragged her in to meet the brand-new husband. Somehow she managed to keep up the pretence of normality, even managing to show a delight in their happiness before making the excuse of not having slept all night and escaping to her bedroom to fall into blessed oblivion as soon as her head touched the pillow.

Exhausted not only by two nights without sleep but by all the emotional turmoil, she almost slept the clock round and the next day she was too busy helping Poppy get ready to fly off to Brussels with her new husband to have time to dwell on her unhappiness.

'You won't be able to keep on your job at Sakers as well,' Poppy said doubtfully when Kirsten told her she was going to try to run the antique shop by herself, if Poppy was agreeable. 'But of course you must realise that. And anyway, you'll have the commission from the sale of Jude's drawings, won't you,' she finished happily.

There didn't seem any point in telling her she would no longer be welcome at the Saker Galleries even if she had wanted to return to her job there, Kirsten thought, or that as there had been no sale of the drawings, there would be no commission either. She could only be grateful that Poppy was so wrapped up in the new life ahead of her that she didn't ask questions or notice how reluctant Kirsten was to talk of her trip to Bermuda.

But when she had finally waved the newly-weds off, the silence of the shop closed round her, and there was all too much time to think, to remember, time to wonder where Benet was and what he was doing, and time incautiously to dream of what might have been. She could only hope that by throwing herself into her work she would gradually be able to forget him.

But only two people came into the shop that day, and only one bought anything. It seemed to set the pattern and by the end of the second week Kirsten was beginning to realise just how helpful her salary from Sakers had been in keeping the shop solvent. If things went on like this she would be hard put to it to find the money for the rent, let alone to put into new stock.

But not even the financial worry of being able to keep a roof over her head could drive the memory of Benet away. At moments when she least expected it he would fill her mind; the terrible memory of his contemptuous turning away from her after he had told Jude he was welcome to her ate into her like corrosive acid. But the happier memories—their joyful, passionate lovemaking, the possessively fierce expression on his face when he'd told her he *did* have to marry her because the thought of her ever marrying someone else was more than he could stand— they were somehow even more painful because they reminded her of all she had lost.

She tried to tell herself a man who had so little trust in her, who doubted her so easily, wasn't worth losing any sleep over, but it was never any use. Her body wouldn't stop aching for him or her heart stop its longing. The evidence against her had been so damning she couldn't really blame him for believing it. The man she loved, the man she wanted more than anything in the world saw her only as a liar and a cheat, and it was something she would have to learn to live with.

Kirsten had heard nothing from her aunt since her return from Bermuda so when, three weeks into struggling to make a go of the antique shop alone, she answered the telephone one evening, she was surprised to recognise Mrs Pattinson's unusually incoherent voice.

'Oh Miss Kirsten—something dreadful! It's your aunt. She was just getting up from the dinner table and she dropped like a stone. Unconscious, she was, and I couldn't move her. Well, you know how heavy she is. I called the doctor and he got the ambulance at once. A stroke, he said it was. A massive stroke. Oh, Miss Kirsten, they took her off and I don't know if she's alive or dead.'

'Now calm down, Patti.' Kirsten felt far from calm herself. Her aunt had always seemed so indestructible it was a shock to realise even she wasn't immune from illness—and perhaps even death. 'Which hospital did they take her to, Patti?'

'The Infirmary, I think. Yes, I'm sure it was. Oh Miss Kirsten, whatever—'

'Now you're not to worry,' Kirsten cut in ruthlessly on her wailing. 'I'll get straight over there and I'll stay until I'm sure what's happening. As soon as I know something I'll phone you, whatever time it is.' Cutting her short when the housekeeper would have gone into even greater detail of her employer's collapse, she put the phone down, grabbed her bag and hurried out to start up the old van, hoping and praying there was enough petrol in the tank to get her to the hospital, as it had become one of her economies to use the van as little as possible. In spite of the years of unloving domination and in spite of her aunt's disgusted repudiation of her that evening on the terrace at Everleigh, it never occurred to Kirsten not to go running the moment her aunt needed her.

She arrived at the hospital to learn her aunt was in intensive care, still undergoing treatment but holding her own, though it was still touch and go. Kirsten spent long weary hours pacing the waiting room and dawn was streaking the sky before a nurse came to tell her she could see her aunt for a few moments. 'Though I'm afraid Miss Douglas won't know you,' she warned.

Kirsten stood looking down at the unmoving body on the high narrow bed. The strong features seemed to have sagged and softened and the many wires and tubes connecting her to the range of machines seemed an indignity somehow when she was so helpless, even though they were saving her life. It wasn't until the nurse touched her arm that she realised tears were running down her cheeks.

'There's nothing you can do here,' the nurse told her. 'So go home and get some rest. We'll phone you if there's any change.'

Kirsten left her number and climbed wearily back into her van, feeling as if the foundations of her world had shifted and slipped yet again. Sparing a thought for the anxious housekeeper, she phoned her a report and fell thankfully into bed to snatch a few hours' sleep.

She rang the hospital as soon as the alarm jangled her awake in the morning and phoned again during the afternoon to be told each time there was no change in her aunt's condition, but when she returned to the hospital to visit that evening she heard that there had been a slight improvement and her aunt had opened her eyes.

It was with some trepidation that Kirsten approached the bed. If her aunt was awake then would seeing the niece she had come to despise do her more harm than good?

She was awake, her eyes wide open staring straight up at the ceiling.

'Hello, Aunt Gussie.' Kirsten's voice trembled, but there was no response from the inert figure on the bed. Even when she leaned across right into her aunt's line of vision there was no reaction. Shocked, she jerked back, and the eyes followed her, though still without a flicker of recognition.

'Hello, Aunt Gussie,' she said again, deliberately moving to one side, and the eyes still followed her.

So she *could* see! Whatever the damage the stroke had done to her aunt's brain, she had some degree of consciousness. Sitting down and taking her aunt's hand she began to talk quietly, telling her not to worry, that Mrs Pattinson was taking care of everything at Lake House and that Aunt Gussie must direct all her efforts into getting well again. She talked about the roses in the garden, even about the antique shop and some of her customers until the lids of the eyes that had never once stopped gazing at her began to droop as her aunt fell asleep.

For the next four visits it was the same, but on the fifth evening the sister met her at the door and told her Miss Douglas had been moved into a private room.

'She's better, then?' Kirsten asked eagerly. 'She can talk? Well enough to be asked to be moved?'

'Oh no, my dear.' The sister looked at her pityingly. 'She no longer needs intensive care but there's still no speech. No, it was Mr Saker who insisted on a private room for her when we told him we were moving her into the ward.'

Kirsten felt as if she had received a blow that knocked all the air out of her lungs. 'He—he's been to see her, then?' she said.

'Oh yes, he's been sitting with her for half an hour most afternoons.' The sister's eyes brightened visibly.

Pain jagged through her. The afternoons, when he could be reasonably certain Kirsten was working and he would be unlikely to even have to pass her in the corridor. Well, she hadn't been able to bring herself to contact *him* to let him know what had happened, had she? She had asked Mrs Pattinson to do it. But still the knowledge that he was deliberately avoiding her hurt.

Over the next couple of weeks there were improvements. It became obvious Aunt Gussie could hear because she began to make slurred noises in response, and she recovered a slight movement in her right hand. But they were very minor improvements and when the doctor asked to see her after an evening visit she was shocked to hear him tell her the hospital had done all they could for her aunt and that as they needed the bed, other arrangements would have to be made for her.

'Such as?' Kirsten prompted.

'Well Mr Saker suggests a nursing home,' the doctor said. 'I expect he's already talked it over with you as it's your decision, being Miss Douglas's next of kin.'

'No. No, he hasn't.' Benet wouldn't demean himself by consulting her. He was treating her as if she didn't exist. Suddenly she was blazingly angry. What right did he have to assume arrogant control? She hadn't argued when he had had Aunt Gussie moved to a private room off his own bat, knowing she herself couldn't possibly have paid for it and being uncertain whether it could be paid for out of her aunt's income now she was helpless. But this was different. Oh, she knew he had a genuine concern for her aunt, but she was also certain it wasn't his only motive. Taking the responsibility for Gussie Douglas on himself would give him another stick to beat her, Kirsten, with. He obviously thought she didn't care about her aunt and would be only too happy to leave her welfare to others, and how he would enjoy sneering at her willing abdication of responsibility!

Well, she *did* care. Curbing her anger with difficulty she asked, 'Doctor, what's the alternative to a nursing home?'

'Taking her back to her own home, of course,' he said promptly. 'Provided there was someone to look after her.'

Kirsten's impulse was to say at once that that was what she would do, but not even her anger at Benet Saker's arrogance could quite make her forget that it wasn't her own feelings that mattered, but what was going to be best for her aunt.

She ran a distraught hand through her hair. 'Doctor,

tell me honestly, is my aunt ever going to get any better than she is now?'

He sighed. 'My dear, I wish I could tell you. She might live on like this for some time or she could have another massive stroke tomorrow. On the other hand, I've known patients as badly affected as your aunt make quite remarkable improvements, especially in the security of their own home and with loving nursing.'

That clinched it as far as Kirsten was concerned. 'Then she must come home,' she said firmly.

The doctor smiled as if that was what he had been hoping to hear, but his voice held a warning as he said, 'It's not going to be easy for you. She'll need constant nursing and it's heavy work. Your aunt's a big woman and there doesn't look enough of you to be a weight-lifter.'

Kirsten lifted her chin. 'I'll manage, and I won't be alone. There's a housekeeper who's been with my aunt for years.'

She had committed herself. It would mean giving up her flat, giving up the business she had been struggling to keep afloat and moving back to Lake House. But what did it matter, she thought wearily. What was she giving up anyway? The business could hardly be said to be flourishing and life without Benet was going to be bleak and arid wherever she lived it.

The next couple of days were very busy. Kirsten wrote to her landlord surrendering her lease on the shop and flat, contacted another dealer and arranged for him to buy her complete stock, then she wrote to Poppy, telling her what she had done and enclosing a cheque for half the proceeds. She saw her aunt's solicitor and bank manager to arrange for the household bills to be paid until such time as her aunt, with luck, would be able to manage her own affairs once again and, finally, she packed all her personal belongings into the old van and transported them back to Lake House before selling the van to the local garage and again sharing the proceeds with Poppy.

And if she regretted giving up her hard-won independence, to hear her aunt's grateful sigh as she was settled into her own bed, and to see her eyes lingering over every detail of the familiar room made it all worthwhile.

The doctor had been right, it *was* hard work, grindingly hard at times, for Aunt Gussie was completely helpless. She had to be fed, washed, changed, massaged against bedsores. Her bedding had to be renewed frequently so her dead weight had to be lifted. Even during the night she needed attention so Kirsten had to set her alarm for every two hours in order to check up on her. Mrs Pattinson helped, of course, but she was no longer young herself and still had the cooking and housekeeping to do, not to mention the extra washing, so most of the nursing Kirsten took on her own small shoulders. But still she found time to read to her aunt regularly from the local paper because she felt it was important to keep her patient's mind alive and interested.

· The telephone had to be answered constantly too during those first few days as Gussie Douglas's friends rang up to find out how she was, but there were no visitors until one afternoon as Kirsten was coming wearily down the stairs with yet another bundle of soiled sheets, the doorbell rang.

'I'll get it, Patti,' she called out, pushing the bundle out of sight under a chair. Without giving a thought to her appearance, indeed unaware that her hair looked lank and lifeless because she hadn't found time to wash it and that her face without make-up was pale and her eyes dark circled from her broken nights, she opened the door.

He was just a dark figure silhouetted against the bright sunlight, but she knew him instantly. Her heart began to thud in her chest and for a moment she dared to hope . . .

'So it *is* true. I couldn't credit it when they told me at the hospital you'd brought Gussie home to look after her yourself.' The jeering note in Benet's voice smothered the fleeting hope and left her trembling inside, fighting too hard not to let him see her distress to attempt a reply.

As if disappointed that she hadn't risen to the bait he went on goadingly. 'Well, you've made your gesture, though I can't think why as I know you don't have a conscience, but now I insist on doing what I wanted to do all along, install your aunt in a nursing home where I know she'll be cared for properly.

The trembling grew worse until she was shaking from head to foot, only now it was with fury. 'You insist! Since when was it any of your business? *I* happen to be Aunt Gussie's next of kin in case you've forgotten, and I'm perfectly capable of seeing she gets proper attention. And if her doctor is satisfied with my efforts, what can it possibly have to do with you?'

His hard jaw thrust out threateningly and his eyes glittered with a cold anger. 'I've made it my business because Gussie Douglas was the nearest I ever came to having a mother during my growing-up years and I want to repay her. And also—' His contemptuous glance raked her. 'Knowing the kind of person you are, I'm not at all happy leaving her to *your* tender mercies.'

The insult bit deep. Even if she hadn't been so convinced her aunt was happier here in her own home, nothing would have induced her to become beholden to a man who was only looking for yet another excuse to hate her.

'You don't even begin to know the kind of person I am, *Mr* Saker,' she ground out. 'And neither do you have the least idea of what is best for my aunt. When the doctor tells me she will be better off in a nursing home, I'll let her go. But not before, so you can go and flourish your cheque-book elsewhere.'

She could almost hear him grinding his teeth. 'And

what does your lover think of your determination to play Florence Nightingale?' he taunted. 'Jude was never one to go in for self-sacrifice. Or is he willing to go along with it for the time being, seeing that you'll be a comparatively rich woman when your aunt dies?'

Her stinging slap caught him by surprise and his eyes held an ugly expression as he put his hand up to the white mark on his cheek that was already beginning to turn red. 'You haven't heard the last of this, Kirsten. I'll get your aunt out of your clutches if it's the last thing I do.' With the threat still hanging in the air between them he turned on his heel and stormed back to his car.

The laughter that shook her already trembling body had a touch of hysteria as she watched the gravel spurt from beneath his tyres. If Benet Saker imagined there was going to be anything for her out of her aunt's estate then he wasn't as well acquainted with Gussie Douglas's affairs as he thought he was. That he should believe her capable of such a mercenary motive made her regret that slap not one whit. Even so, the violence of his threat made her uneasy.

It preyed on her mind and she couldn't help wondering if someone with the kind of power and influence Benet Saker had *would* find a way to over-ride her own wishes, and when, a couple of days later when she was just going out into the garden to pick some roses for her aunt's room, she found him getting out of his car, she flew at him like a tigress.

'You're wasting your time. You are *not* going to put Aunt Gussie away in any nursing home. She may be completely helpless but she *is* very aware of her surroundings. So whatever you're planning I'll tell you now; nothing will induce me to agree to shuffle her off to a strange place I know she would hate.'

His eyes widened and he looked taken aback at her tirade, but his voice was cold when he retorted, 'If you don't mind I'd like to see for myself how comfortably situated she is here.'

Kirsten's back was rigid as she led the way upstairs, but pushing open the door of the room she momentarily forgot the man behind her as she found her aunt had slipped into an uncomfortable position while the book Kirsten had left on her lap had fallen to the floor. One of her triumphs over the last few days had been that Aunt Gussie could now turn over the pages of a book and look at the pictures even if she couldn't read the text.

'Oh dear, have you lost your book?' Answering the appeal in her aunt's eyes she heaved her forward over her shoulder, straightened the pillows and heaved her aunt's dead weight back against them, panting from the effort as she straightened up. 'You won't need your book for a little while, Aunt. Look, you have a visitor.' The pleasure her aunt managed to convey when she saw Benet was unmistakable.

Angry and hurt though she was, Kirsten had to acknowledge that for her, that terrible tug of attraction was as powerful as ever and that his callous treatment of her hadn't killed her love for him, so when she went downstairs to make some tea she lingered longer than necessary, reluctant to spend any more time than necessary in his company. She was careful not to put a cup for herself on the tray and while Benet drank his, she concentrated on her aunt, folding the partially useful hand round the spouted drinking cup so that her patient shouldn't feel absolutely helpless, but holding it there with her own as she helped her to drink.

At last Benet got up to go, and after taking an affectionate farewell of her aunt and promising to come again he said stiffly. 'I'd like a word with you, Kirsten, before I go.'

She gathered up the teacups and walked out of the room ahead of him, carrying the tray. Still holding it as a form of defence she turned in the hall to say, 'Well?'

His face was stiff, his eyes directed somewhere above her head. 'Much as it goes against the grain, I have to admit Gussie *would* be happier staying put—'

Kirsten let out a long breath of surprise.

'—on the condition that you let me provide you with a nurse.'

The china rattled as her hands shook. 'And for a moment I almost believed you were giving me a vote of confidence! But you still can't admit I'm capable of nursing my aunt, can you, or that I should *want* to do it?'

'You may think you're indestructable,' he said harshly, 'but you're not. You can't go on lifting Gussie about like that on your own.'

Her eyes widened. 'You're making the offer out of concern for me?'

He turned and walked to the door, saying over his shoulder, 'I'm thinking of your aunt. I'll have to get a nurse in if you crack up, and it would be better if it was one she already knew.'

Kirsten's heart contracted painfully.

The nurse arrived two days later, escorted by Benet. She heard their shared laughter and watched Benet usher her into the house, his arm around her shoulders, smiling down at the pretty, upturned face. But when he looked up and saw Kirsten his smile vanished and she had to clutch at the banister rail at the intensity of her hurt.

'Susan, this is Kirsten Douglas, your patient's niece,' Benet said formally. 'I'm sure you'll be able to come to an amicable agreement about sharing the workload.' And then as an afterthought, 'Susan Wendell, Kirsten.'

Somehow Kirsten managed to make it down the rest of the stairs and held out her hand. 'I'm pleased you could come, Nurse Wendell.'

'Oh, Susan, please,' the nurse said, her smile wide and friendly. She was young, probably no older than Kirsten herself, blonde and very pretty and it was obvious she had fallen victim to Benet's charm. But even while jealousy curdled inside her, Kirsten couldn't help but respond to the girl's open friendliness.

'And you must call me Kirsten. I must say it'll be a relief to have some help. It's the broken nights that are so wearing.'

'I don't want all the night duty put on Susan,' Benet said sharply, and Kirsten winced. No, of course he didn't, she thought. He would want to be able to visit Aunt Gussie and be reasonably certain he wouldn't have to endure her own hateful presence. He might even have ideas of filling in some of the nurse's spare evenings himself.

It seemed that she was right because Benet became a very regular visitor, not only coming to see her aunt most afternoons, but often dropping in again in the evenings too, and that Susan was the attraction was only too painfully obvious as most of his evening visits were to see her or to take her out. Kirsten tried to avoid him as much as possible, finding something to do elsewhere whenever he was with her aunt and sitting in the sickroom while Susan was entertaining him downstairs. But it was impossible to stay out of his way altogether, especially when Mrs Pattinson began asking him to stay for meals. And it was sheer torture for Kirsten having to watch him being so charming and flirtatious with Susan while the few remarks he addressed to herself were cruelly needling and coldly contemptuous.

It was a particularly cruel remark that prompted her first fainting attack—at least, that was what Kirsten put it down to at the time. Benet had come to see her aunt in the late morning and had stayed to lunch. As they were rising from the table he said playfully to Susan, 'You're losing the roses in your cheeks, my girl. Come out with me for a drive this afternoon. We'll go to Glastonbury and you can blow the cobwebs away climbing the Tor.'

'Oh, that sounds like heaven! Would you mind, Kirsten?' Susan said hopefully.

Kirsten minded very much. Not only had Benet never considered herself in need of a break, but he seemed to be taking a positive delight in conducting his new love affair before her eyes. But all she said was, 'Well I *had* hoped to catch up on some sleep this afternoon.'

'You never used to sleep in the afternoon,' Benet reminded her cruelly. 'Though I do remember you being only too happy to spend it in bed.'

She felt her face drain of colour and the breath rasped hoarsely in her throat while the room swung round her. Too proud to tell him she needed to rest because she had spent last night in the sickroom with her aunt who hadn't been so well, she clung to the back of a chair, managing to say, 'By all means go out for a while, Susan,' closing her eyes so the room didn't move around so dizzily, holding on until they had both left the room before dropping to the floor in a faint.

It hadn't lasted long and Kirsten blamed it on lack of sleep and the strain she had been under, but the second time it happened she was in the bath. Luckily she managed to scramble out before collapsing on the floor or she might have drowned, and this time when she came round she was violently sick.

Although she didn't faint again, the sickness seemed to come back each morning and it was a sudden appalled suspicion that sent her riffling through the pages of her diary. It was true. So much had happened since she came back from Bermuda that she hadn't noticed the missed period. That afternoon of abandoned passion in the beach house was to have consequences she ought to have forgotten but hadn't. She was pregnant.

CHAPTER NINE

The diary fell from Kirsten's fingers and she slumped on to her bed, utterly crushed by this new catastrophe. She was going to have Benet's child! Dear God, what was she going to do?

But her mind seemed incapable of rational thought, could only scream out a soundless denial. *It can't be true* . . . Fate surely couldn't be so cruel. Another bout of sickness sent her rushing for the bathroom, as if underlining the very fact she was trying to deny. When she finally emerged, white and shivering, it was to collide with Susan, knocking the spongebag out of the nurse's hand.

Susan eyed her sharply. 'Kirsten, are you all right? You do look ropy.'

Kirsten managed a smile and retrieved the spongebag. 'Must be something I ate, but I'm feeling much better now,' she lied, and escaped thankfully to her room where she sat shivering on the bed, trying to come to terms with her predicament, but still unable to face the reality of it.

Any child of that rapturous union in the beach house should have been lapped in love from the moment of conception, wanted and cherished by both loving parents—not handicapped by illegitimacy, not born to a mother who was hated and despised by its father.

Great shudders shook her body as she realised how much more he was going to hate and despise her now. It didn't take much imagination to visualise his contemptuous rage when she told him. And she would have to tell him, she realised with a quailing spirit, for how was she going to provide for this child without his help? For as long as Aunt Gussie lived and needed her there would be a home for her here, but how much longer would that be? Her aunt's grip on life was tenuous—hadn't the doctor warned of the danger of another stroke that could be fatal? And might not the anger and disgust at the shame Kirsten had brought on them be enough to cause that fatal collapse once Kirsten's condition became impossible to hide from her? Not only would she have her aunt's death on her conscience, she would no longer have a roof over her head. She would have no job and no money to provide for the child's future.

But aside from all the practical problems of her dilemma, didn't Benet have a right to know she had conceived his child, however unwelcome the news might be? And didn't she have an obligation, for the child's sake, to accept his help, however reluctantly given? Somehow she had to find the courage to tell him.

It was the longest day Kirsten had ever lived through, her ears strained for the sound of his car coming up the drive, and then she might have missed him had she not taken the precaution of asking Mrs Pattinson to tell him she would like to speak to him. She was coming in from hanging yet another batch of bed linen out to dry in the sun as the housekeeper returned to the kitchen with the afternoon tea tray and told her Benet was waiting for her in the drawing room.

Now the moment had come, her heart hammered with apprehension and she had to force down the suddenly welling nausea as she crossed the hall. But she stopped dead in the drawing room doorway, for Benet was not alone. Susan was standing very close to him, smiling up at him flirtatiously saying, 'Till seven-thirty tonight, then.'

Susan had her back to Kirsten, but Benet was facing her and she was sure he had seen her. Quite deliberately he pulled the pretty nurse into his arms and kissed her lingeringly. Incapable of moving, incapable, too, of hiding the tearing hurt she felt, Kirsten could only watch as Benet reluctantly let the other girl go.

'The rest will have to wait till tonight,' he told Susan with a teasing smile. 'We have company.'

The nurse whirled round, her face crimson, her embarrassment acute as she murmured an excuse and left the room.

Benet didn't move, and certainly he showed no embarrassment himself. 'What's the matter, Kirsten? Piqued because I've found consolation?' he taunted, as if he was actually enjoying the hurt she knew she had betrayed. 'At least Susan doesn't have some devious scheme to seduce me. How is your lover, by the way? I must say I'm surprised at his patience. Or do you manage to slip away back to him every now and then to keep him satisfied?'

Her face chalk-white, perspiration beading her upper lip as she struggled to hold down the sickness that gripped her, Kirsten could only stare at him mutely.

As if annoyed by her lack of response Benet said irritably, 'Oh, forget it. What did you want to see me about?'

Kirsten opened her mouth to speak, but no words came. What was the use? If Benet still believed Jude was her lover would he believe the child she was carrying was his? Wouldn't he accuse her of further trickery, trying to foist the paternity on him? He hadn't believed the truth before and his taunt about her supposed relationship with his half-brother didn't lead her to suppose he would believe her now, so why put herself through the pain and humiliation of trying to convince him? There would be no help for her from this quarter. Her baby was a problem she would have to cope with alone.

'Nothing. It was nothing,' she managed, turning away and running upstairs so abruptly she didn't see his face whiten as he glimpsed the naked despair on hers.

Kirsten lived doggedly from day to day, moving like an automaton about her duties, finding it difficult to eat because of the constant nausea and impossible to sleep for the nagging worry about the future. She began to lose weight so rapidly that taking her turn in the sickroom became an enormous effort, and often she dissolved into helpless tears of exhaustion.

As if she didn't have enough to bear, the slight improvement her aunt had made since being brought back to Lake House seemed to be slipping away. The restless eyes followed Kirsten's movements less often and she lost all interest in trying to turn the pages of a book or in making the pretence of feeding herself. The doctor warned that the end might not be long in coming and while the knowledge brought a regretful sadness, Kirsten couldn't deny a certain relief at the thought that her aunt's sufferings might be over without her ever having to know the disgrace Kirsten had brought upon herself.

So great was Kirsten's preoccupation with the sheer effort of getting through each succeeding day she could no longer find the spirit to rise to Benet's taunts or even to notice when the taunts ceased. When he rebuked her for not eating enough to keep a bird alive she merely bowed her head to hide her haunted eyes while she struggled to force a few more mouthfuls down her constricted throat, and so missed his sharp look of grudging concern.

His invitation to go for a drive with him one afternoon did surprise her, but supposing his motive was only to drag up painful accusations again and knowing if he did, she would almost certainly break down, she quietly refused, suggesting he took Susan instead.

And later that afteroon, sitting with her aunt, Kirsten was glad she had refused. It happened so quickly, a convulsive jerk of the limbs that had lain inert for so many weeks, a long, rasping breath and then an uncanny stillness. Even as her shaking fingers dialled the doctor's number she knew it was too late for him to help Aunt Gussie now.

Waiting for the doctor who promised to come at once, she stood by the bed feeling desperately alone. Aunt Gussie had never loved her, but at least she had been family. Now there was no one. Aunt Gussie had gone, Poppy, engrossed with her new husband was abroad and Benet, whose love and support she needed so desperately, could only feel revulsion and hatred for her. The sound of a car brought her out of her bitter reverie and with a feeling of unreality she went downstairs.

'Benet's right behind me,' the doctor said, bustling past her without stopping. 'I overtook him like a bat out of hell so he'll know there's something up. Stay here and break it to him, will you?'

He hadn't reached the top of the stairs before Benet's car drew up with a flurry of gravel and he leapt out. 'What's the matter? Why's the doctor here?'

'Aunt Gussie—she—she's—' But suddenly the shock of coping with her aunt's death alone on top of the debilitating weeks of emotional turmoil and worry was too much. Her hold on reality slipped and she thankfully slid into a black pit of oblivion.

Something pungent caught at the back of her throat making her gasp. She tried to twist away but there was no escaping it. Slowly the blackness receded and she found herself lying on her bed with Susan bending over her, holding smelling salts under her nose.

'She's coming round,' Susan said as Kirsten pushed the evil smelling bottle away, and one of the two figures who appeared to be arguing by the window detached itself and came nearer.

'Thank God for that!' A muscle twitched in Benet's jaw. 'The doctor's just been tearing a strip off me, and he's quite right. I should never have left you alone in the house when I knew this could happen.'

Kirsten closed her eyes against the sudden longing for it to be concern for herself that prompted his self-castigation, but she knew he had only been thinking of her aunt. 'You couldn't have done anything for her, even if you had been here,' she said weakly. 'It happened so quickly, not even the doctor could have helped.'

'That may be true, but it doesn't stop *me* feeling guilty,' Susan said. 'I was being paid to be there in just such an emergency. Now let me put you to bed properly so you can get some rest. You frightened us to death dropping at our feet like that.'

'You've been pushing yourself too hard for too long,' Benet broke in harshly.

Kirsten looked up at him. If only he would show her just a little kindness, but the planes of his face could have been carved from stone.

'I can't. There's so much to do. The undertakers—the funeral—so many people to tell . . .' She struggled to sit up but hard hands gripped her shoulders roughly and thrust her back.

'My God but you're stubborn! Doctor, isn't there something you can give her to knock her out?'

'Benet's right, my dear.' The kindly doctor loomed over her from the other side of the bed and before she realised what he intended, she felt the prick of the needle in her arm. 'You've stood as much as your nervous system will take and you must have some rest. So stop worrying and let the sedative take its course. I'm sure you can safely leave the funeral arrangements to Benet.'

Kirsten slept almost solidly for two days and two nights, waking only briefly for Susan to help her to the bathroom and to take the tempting invalid food Mrs Pattinson sent up for her on a tray and then sliding back into sleep again as if she could never get enough of it.

On the third morning she woke early feeling refreshed and better than she had for a long while. Without waiting for Susan's ministrations she got up and took a leisurely bath and washed her hair, and had just finished drying it when the other girl came into the room.

'You're feeling better? Oh, that's marvellous!' Susan said with genuine pleasure.

Kirsten smiled. 'Yes thanks, much better.' And it really was amazing what the hours of rest and natural sleep, the release from tension, the sheer relief of escaping Benet's condemning eyes had done for her optimism. Her biggest worries—her uncertain future and her fears for her unborn child—were still there, of course, but this morning she had managed to push them to the back of her mind. This morning even the anguish of knowing she was irrevocably committed to a man who could only see her as a liar and a cheat had lost its savagery, blunted to a dull ache.

She would never forget him, not when she had his child as a constant reminder, but perhaps when she no longer had to see him, no longer had to face his bitter contempt, she would be able to forget the pain of his rejection, maybe even lose her hopeless longing for him and remember only the brief happiness they had shared. She would still have to see him at the funeral, but with so many people there their contact must of necessity be mere social politeness. And then it would all be over. She could begin again, begin to build a new life for herself—and her baby.

'I'm sorry you had all the trouble of looking after me when I'm sure you could have done with a rest yourself.' Kirsten squeezed Susan's hand. 'But thanks, anyway.'

'Nonsense. I wanted to stay for your aunt's funeral and having something to do made me feel I wasn't drawing my pay for nothing. Besides—' Susan grimaced '—Benet would have had my guts for garters if I *hadn't* taken care of you.'

'Benet?' Kirsten stared at her disbelievingly, her hairbrush poised in mid-air. Then she shook her head, knowing it couldn't be true.

Susan took the brush out of her hand. 'You know your hair really is a glorious colour,' she said, sliding the bristles gently through the coppery mass.

Kirsten tugged at a curl straggling into her eyes. 'It needs cutting.'

'Oh, I don't know . . .' Susan stood back critically. 'This length suits you if the front is trimmed a bit. Have you got some scissors?'

Kirsten passed her a pair from the dressing table drawer and submitted while the other girl snipped. 'There,' Susan said with satisfaction.

Kirsten stared at her reflection. It was the first time she had taken any notice of her appearance for weeks and it was almost like looking at a stranger. All trace of the tan she had acquired in Bermuda had gone and her face was pale, the skin almost translucent. More than forty-eight hours of sleep had removed the dark circles from under her eyes, but the weeks of strain had hollowed out the childish roundness of her cheeks bringing her cheekbones into prominence, but the longer hair curling in her neck softened the new, sharper line of her jaw and the short fronds Susan had left over her forehead made her eyes look enormous.

'A bit of make-up today, don't you think?' Susan encouraged, and while Kirsten applied a slick of bronze shadow to her eyelids, outlined her mouth with a pale coral lipstick and flicked blusher over her cheeks to give herself a bit of spurious colour, Susan went to the wardrobe and selected a dress for her to wear. It was one of the sun-dresses she had worn in Bermuda as the wisps of early morning mist were already clearing and it promised to be a hot day, but when Kirsten slipped it on she was conscious of the weight she must have lost since she last wore it, the wide neckline revealing a new boniness in her shoulders and the belt needing to be cinched in at least another two holes.

Well, perhaps now that that dreadful nausea had left her—as it seemed to have done—she would have more appetite and would be able to put back some of her former curves. Still with that new feeling of optimism Kirsten led the way downstairs, her face alight with laughter at some remark of Susan's as she pushed open the breakfast room door.

A tall figure rose from his seat at the table, a strange expression in the vivid blue eyes that raked over her.

'Benet!' Her laughter died like a light being extinguished and she saw his jaw harden, bringing a return of the tension to the pit of her stomach.

'Oh, you didn't know Benet has moved into the house temporarily, did you?' Susan said, blithely unaware of the fraught atmosphere. 'It seemed the best thing to do when there was so much to arrange.'

'Of course. I'm sorry I had to leave it all on your shoulders, Benet,' Kirsten said stiltedly, taking her place opposite him, but not allowing her gaze to rise higher than his tie. 'When is the funeral?'

'Tomorrow morning at eleven-thirty.' His voice was crisp and businesslike. 'Mrs Pattinson is laying on a buffet lunch for anyone who cares to come back to the house afterwards.'

Kirsten closed her eyes. Another—what? Thirty hours before she would see him for the last time? Thirty hours of close contact she hadn't bargained for. The old familiar nausea rose up in her throat, killing her new-found appetite.

Somehow she managed to get through the day, retreating to the kitchen to help with the preparations for what Mrs Pattinson insisted on calling 'the wake', in spite of Susan's protests at her working and Benet's tight-lipped support of the nurse.

The funeral itself passed in a blur, just isolated impressions remaining with her afterwards; the lump in her throat that so many people should have turned out to pay their last respects to her aunt; the heavy scent of the lilies in the flower arrangement close by the front pew where she sat alone which gave her a headache and brought on a bout of nausea that beaded her paper-white face with perspiration as she struggled not to disgrace herself; the relief so great at being in the open air again that she hardly noticed it was Benet's hand that helped her across the rough ground to the graveside; and Benet himself, standing beside her as the vicar intoned the committal prayers, so darkly handsome, so attractive and yet so remote.

A sizeable crowd of people followed them back to the house afterwards for the buffet lunch and there was some release from tension for Kirsten as she circulated among the guests, the sheer number of them helping her to avoid Benet. Now the time for the parting of the ways was drawing close she was trying not to think about it. While part of her longed to be free of the pain of seeing him constantly, another part of her dreaded the moment when he would walk out of her life forever.

As the guests began to disperse, Mr Branscombe, her aunt's solicitor, took her arm. 'Kirsten, my dear, I'd like to talk to you rather urgently.'

'About the will, I suppose?' Kirsten tried to show an interest. 'Do you need anyone else? Mrs Pattinson? Benet? I'm sure they're all beneficiaries.'

'Oh no, I don't want a formal reading,' he said hastily. 'But if there's somewhere you and I could be private?'

Kirsten glanced around the thinning numbers in the hall, even the stragglers now making their way to the door where Benet was seeing them off. She saw him looking at her, saw his sardonic glance and knew exactly what he was thinking, that now was the pay-off, now she was about to get her reward. She turned her back on him. 'The breakfast room, I think, Mr Branscombe.'

The solicitor opened his briefcase and when Kirsten was seated opposite he took out a folded sheet of heavy paper. 'Your aunt's will—' he said. 'Your aunt has made a number of bequests, modest ones to Mrs Pattinson and to Betts, the gardener, a rather less modest one to the church and a sizeable one—all her antique furniture and silver, porcelain and pictures—to Benet Saker. The residue she leaves to you, but I'm afraid, my dear, that isn't quite what it seems. You see—'

'The residue being this house which was no longer hers to bequeath,' Kirsten broke in calmly. 'Yes, she told me several weeks ago Lake House would become the property of an insurance company on her death.'

'She told you?' Mr Branscombe looked taken aback. 'Well, I suppose that makes my job a fraction less unpleasant. My dear, I'm sorry. Time and time again I tried to talk her into making better provision for you, but she seemed to have the idea that you would be married and settled comfortably long before this situation would arise. She even hinted that Benet Saker would be the lucky man.' His voice rose questioningly. 'I take it that's not the case?'

Her face flaming, pain twisting and jerking inside her, Kirsten shook her head. 'There's not the remotest possibility.'

Mr Branscombe didn't hide his disappointment. 'Pity. But at least if you and Benet were close enough for your aunt to have harboured such hopes, it makes what I am about to suggest a feasible proposition. As I said, Benet is by the far the biggest beneficiary and he is already a rich man. So my advice to you is to contest the will. I'm sure you'll find Benet will agree you've been most unfairly treated, and that he will also agree to a more equitable division of your aunt's property.'

Kirsten almost laughed aloud. She knew very well Benet would *not* agree, in fact he would believe she had got her just deserts. And rather than have him know and so give him yet another opportunity to crow over her, she said quickly, 'No, Mr Branscombe. I'm sure you mean well but I have no intention of contesting anything. This is how my aunt wished to leave her property and I have no quarrel with it.'

'But, my dear girl, I do beg you to reconsider,' the solicitor pleaded earnestly. 'Without the valuable items specifically left to Benet, there's going to be virtually nothing left for you. Certainly no more than a few hundred pounds.'

For a moment Kirsten's heart quailed. So little! For herself it didn't matter, but when she had the baby to consider . . . Even so, she knew that to contest the will would only confirm Benet's already low opinion of her integrity and would draw her into even more hurtful verbal battles with him.

'Benet Saker has been close to my aunt all his life,' she said with quiet dignity. 'Closer to her than I ever was. No, Mr Branscombe, I won't go against my aunt's last wishes. Besides,' she added with a confidence she couldn't truly feel, 'I'm perfectly capable of earning my own living.'

Even as he took his leave at the front door the worried solicitor made a final attempt to persuade her to change her mind. 'Won't you at least discuss it informally with Benet?' he asked, but she shook her head firmly.

'Quite frankly, Mr Branscombe, I'd rather Benet didn't know anything about it.'

'Didn't know what?' a hatefully taunting voice said behind her and she spun round with a gasp, wondering how much he had overheard. 'Just how much loot you've reaped? If it was advice on what to do with your windfall Branscombe was urging you to discuss with me, I'm sure Jude will have his own ideas about that, because that's where you'll be going, isn't it, now you're not only free but rich? Back to your lover.'

Kirsten swayed. How could he still insist that she and Jude had been lovers when at the beach house that day he must have known he was the first? If he could cling to such a belief against the evidence of his own knowledge of her then she was even more fiercely glad she hadn't allowed Mr Branscombe to persuade her into throwing herself on Benet's mercy, because she knew he had none. Even more determined than ever that he would never know that far from being rich, she had somehow got to earn a living for herself and his child, she decided the quickest and least painful way to end this scene was to confirm his belief.

'Yes, that's right,' she agreed stonily.

For just a moment it was as if his face fell into the lines of a man tortured beyond endurance, but the impression was gone so quickly, masked by a cold indifference, that she knew she must have imagined it.

But at least the knowledge that in all these weeks he hadn't softened towards her one iota made it easier to face this parting of the ways. 'I suppose you'll be leaving now.' Annoyed with herself at the betraying catch in her voice in spite of her resolve, she walked past him to the stairs, frozen into sudden immobility when he said harshly, 'I'm afraid your gracious farewell is a little premature. I shall be staying on here tonight—with my hostess's permission, of course.' He sketched a mocking bow. 'I've already arranged to drive Susan back to London tomorrow.'

Kirsten was tempted to order him out there and then. After all, he wasn't to know the house didn't now belong to her. But she didn't. Somehow she managed an indifferent shrug and continued upstairs.

The solicitor had told her that the insurance company would give her reasonable time to make other arrangements before they took possession of Lake House and Kirsten looked forward to a few days' respite, a few days alone without Benet there to churn her emotions, a few days to think, to plan what she should do next. In the event, even this respite was denied her.

The following morning her nausea was so intense and the need to get to the bathroom so urgent she didn't have time to lock the door behind her. It was there that Susan found her, retching helplessly.

When at last, after the nurse's ministrations with a cold wet sponge, Kirsten began to feel better, Susan said gently, 'This isn't the first time, is it? Fainting—morning sickness—Kirsten, are you pregnant?'

Sinking on to the edge of the bath Kirsten nodded weakly, and replying to the nurse's next question, 'Nearly three months.'

'And the father?' Susan probed. 'Does he know?'

Kirsten stood up, suddenly aware of how much she had given away. 'No. And he's not going to either. It's no business of his.'

'Oh, but surely . . .' Susan protested. 'He has a right to know, doesn't he? He'd want to help you, even if he can't marry you.'

'I don't need his help. I don't need anybody's help. Just leave me alone, can't you.' She knew she was being unforgivably rude, but as she pushed past Susan and rushed back to her room she was too panic-stricken to care.

Suppose, just suppose, Susan let slip in front of Benet what she had just learned. They would be breakfasting together shortly before their trip back to London and, from the worried look on the other girl's face, it was possible she might betray the confidence.

For just a few weak moments she wondered perhaps if it wouldn't be better to wait and see what Benet's reaction would be when he learned of her pregnancy and realised he must be responsible for it. But would he? She remembered with sickening clarity that it had been only yesterday that Benet had accused her yet again of being Jude's lover. Wouldn't he be more likely to believe the baby she was expecting was his half-brother's, not his own?

Kirsten began to dress with frantic haste. She couldn't take any more. Hearing Benet rejecting his own child would be the last straw, it would break her. There was only one avenue left open to her—she would have to disappear fast.

Throwing clothes into two small suitcases because they would be easier to manage than one large one, she discarded things like evening dresses that she would no longer have any use for and remembered to include skirts and sweaters against the coming autumn, finally throwing her heavy winter coat around her shoulders even though the day was warm.

A quick check through her handbag confirmed that she had enough money for her train fare and that her bank book was there, though the balance—her share of the proceeds after the dissolution of the partnership with Poppy—suddenly seemed pitifully small when it was all she had between her and destitution.

Cautiously she opened her bedroom door and listened. The upper rooms were silent, and as she crept to the head of the stairs she was relieved to hear Benet's deep voice followed by Susan's lighter tones coming from the breakfast room. Holding her breath and praying Mrs Pattinson wouldn't suddenly emerge from the kitchen and see her, she tiptoed down the stairs, across to the front door and out of the house, closing it with a soft but very final click behind her.

Four hours later she was unpacking her toilet things and a nightdress in the dingy room of a small backstreet hotel and for the first time that day Kirsten felt able to relax. It didn't matter now if Susan betrayed her confidence to Benet. She was safe from his cruel accusations, lost among the teeming population of London.

CHAPTER TEN

THE group of girls who worked nearest to Kirsten in the big open-plan office had their heads together chirruping like cockney sparrows as they hung over something spread out on one of the desks, but the chattering was cut off in mid-breath when Kirsten quietly took her place at her own desk and uncovered her typewriter. After guarded looks at her the conversation continued, now in hissed whispers, until one of the girls detached herself from the group and came across, holding a folded newspaper.

'I say, Kirsten, this wouldn't be you, would it?' The paper was thrust under Kirsten's nose and a finger pointed to an item in the personal column someone had drawn a ring round. 'Look, it says, "Would Miss Kirsten Douglas, formerly of Lake House, Wiston Green, Somerset and now believed to be in London, please contact Mr Branscombe of Branscombe, Bowyer and Seton urgently" and then it gives the address.'

Kirsten felt the colour flood into her face and then ebb away again as she stared at the print dancing before her eyes.

'It *is* you they mean, isn't it?' another of the girls said as they all gathered round her. 'I can tell by the guilty look on your face.'

'Oooh, Kirsten, what *have* you been up to,' another teased, but more out of curiosity than malice.

She could understand their curiosity. They were a friendly enough bunch of girls, but Kirsten had never joined in their constant gossip about boys and she knew they thought her stand-offish. But the last thing she wanted was to start them gossiping about her, so she forced a smile.

'Nothing so very terrible, though I'm ashamed he's had to go to all this trouble to find me,' she said, and went on, sticking to the truth but by no means telling all of it, 'This Mr Branscombe was an old friend of my aunt and I promised to let him have my address when I moved to London after she died a month ago, but I'm afraid it slipped my mind.'

'Is that all?' It was obvious they were disappointed by her prosaic explanation.

'I was sure somebody had died and left you a fortune,' one of them said.

'No chance.' Kirsten grimaced, knowing full well the truth of that. 'I expect that not hearing from me, he's afraid I'm in trouble. He's only interested in knowing whether I found a job and somewhere to live.'

To her relief the supervisor loomed into view and the girls drifted back to their desks. Kirsten fixed the earpiece of her audio machine, switched on the tape and began to type. But it was impossible to concentrate on her work. Mr Branscombe's appeal to her to get in touch had shocked her out of the numbed feeling of unreality that had gripped her since she had fled from Lake House to the anonymity of London just over a month ago.

She had written to the solicitor from the tatty little hotel where she had spent the first two nights, to tell him she had left Lake House and to promise she would contact him again as soon as she had a permanent address, but somehow she had never got round to it, perhaps because the idea that the lonely attic room with peeling walls in bed-sitter land should from now on be her permanent home was just too depressing. And then there had been the worry of finding a job in order to continue paying the rent of the horrible little room. For days she had tramped the streets, following up every possible 'situations vacant' in the newspaper before landing this one as an audio typist in a large, impersonal office block. The work, transcribing statistical reports, required great concentration and accuracy and yet was deadly boring, and although it paid reasonably well, Kirsten had been horrified at the large chunk rent and daily tube fares took out of her weekly pay packet.

It was a constant worry, the need to save, save, save towards the time when she would no longer be able to work, the time when she would have another mouth besides her own to feed. Not that she had been eating very much herself. With rent for her room and the fares to and from work an unavoidable expense, food was the only area where it was possible to make some economies.

But if her days had been filled with the obsession to save for a future she still couldn't really believe in, a future beset by problems so insuperable she couldn't even begin to make plans, her nights had been filled with dreams of Benet, dreams so vivid she would wake shaken by sobbing and filled with a longing time did nothing to blunt.

But now this voice from the past had shaken her out of her inertia. Mr Branscombe must have some news for her. It was strange that she should have forgotten her promise to keep in touch with him, considering how money—or rather the lack of it—loomed so importantly in her life now. The few hundred pounds which he had told her was all she could expect from her aunt's estate took on the aspect of a small fortune.

Before she left the office for her lunch break she wrote to him, giving him her address, and posted it with a sense of anticipation, promising herself that as soon as she had his reply she would begin to make plans for the future, make some arrangements about ante-natal care, find out what help she could get as an unmarried mother.

But thinking about the baby reminded her unbearably

of Benet, and almost without realising it, she found her steps taking her that lunchtime to the part of Mayfair where Benet had his main gallery. She walked slowly along the street, pausing opposite to gaze at the elegant façade of the Saker Galleries. Pain slashed through her with the cutting edge of broken glass. If Jude hadn't used her so callously in his bitter feud with his half-brother, she and Benet would have been married by now. She would have had the support of a husband instead of having to struggle on alone, and her baby would have had an assured future with two loving parents instead of a future so uncertain Kirsten wasn't even sure she would be able to keep him.

Him. Funny, but she had always seen her baby as a boy, a miniature replica of Benet, the same blue eyes, the same dark hair. Her hands went protectively to her stomach, still only a very little distended, but then on her frugal diet she had become painfully thin.

And suddenly she knew that, whatever the difficulties, however insuperable they seemed, she *was* going to keep him, bring him up herself. Her baby was all she had, her reason for living. He would be a little bit of Benet no one would ever take away from her.

Tears blurring her vision she turned away, plunging into the narrow, twisting streets of Shepherd Market and then out into the crowds hurrying along Piccadilly, knowing that the sound echoing in her head of someone calling her name was only imagination.

Two nights later, Kirsten toiled up the steep stairs to her attic room, late because she had stopped off from work at the local health centre and filled with guilt because the receptionist there had been sharp with her for leaving it four months before getting any ante-natal care, underlining her disapproval by giving Kirsten an emergency appointment for the following evening. It was gloomy on the top floor, lit only by a skylight, and Kirsten thought she was hallucinating as she reached the landing and saw a tall, dark figure standing beside her door.

She stopped dead as Benet said harshly, 'Kirsten! For God's sake why did you run off from Lake House like that without telling anyone where you were going? Why didn't you tell me there was nothing left for you out of your aunt's estate?'

Kirsten was shaking with shock, but she managed to fling up her head proudly. 'When you'd made it only too clear my problems were no concern of yours?'

'Oh, but I think they are,' he ground out, and his blue eyes seemed to burn with a murderous rage as they went to her stomach.

He knew about the baby! Kirsten folded her arms protectively over the precious burden she carried. He knew about the baby and now he knew where she lived. He was going to hound her until the baby was born and then he was going to take it away from her because he'd consider her unfit to look after it. She was past thinking logically. She only knew she had to escape from this new threat that even now was advancing on her. Forgetting she was standing at the top of the stairs she whirled round to run and stepped out into space.

The blackness was safe. If she just let herself float in it she need never feel pain or fear or anguish again. But each time she let go, each time she willed herself to float away, something held on to her hands, dragging her back. She tried to fight it, that will that was stronger than her own, but inexorably the comforting blackness lightened to be shot through with pain, with dreams that were even more agonising, dreams where Benet was telling her he loved her, but where every time the love in his eyes would turn to contempt as Jude's red-bearded face jeered.

She finally broke the surface of consciousness to find herself in a strange room. The sudden brightness dazzled her and she closed her eyes again, but the realisation that she couldn't move panicked her into opening them again. Blinking a few times to accustom herself to the light she saw that one of her wrists was encased in a plaster cast and a drip was attached to the vein at her elbow. And she saw, too, that she wasn't alone in the small room. Benet was sitting on a hard chair beside her bed, both his hands clasping one of hers, his head buried on his outstretched arms, apparently asleep.

She tried to move her hand away from his grasp but she was too weak. But he must have felt some movement because his head was suddenly raised and he looked straight into her open eyes.

'It was you,' she thought, 'dragging me back. Haven't you punished me enough?' A thin thread of a voice seemed to echo her thoughts and she realised she had spoken them aloud.

She realised, too, there were tears in his eyes and his face was working convulsively, but then his image began to waver and shimmer and finally disappeared.

The next time Kirsten woke she was alone. The chair Benet had been sitting on was over by the wall. Or had he really been there at all? Perhaps she had dreamed it. Her accusation and his surprising reaction to it must have been a figment of her fevered imagination.

Between sleeping and waking and the ministrations of a nurse who kept assuring her she must rest and not worry, Kirsten lay there in limbo, refusing to let herself think or remember. And then the nurse was back, jollying her along, washing her face, brushing her hair.

Kirsten submitted listlessly until the nurse said, 'Come on, perk up now, Miss Douglás. You're going to have a visitor. Mr Saker will be here in a minute.'

Kirsten stiffened in panic. 'No. Tell him I don't want to see him.'

The nurse looked shocked. 'You can't mean that! Why

he's sat here solidly for two nights and a day. We only persuaded him to get some rest when you'd recovered consciousness and were sleeping naturally. You've been very ill, Miss Douglas. Oh, not from your injuries. But you were so undernourished and debilitated you didn't seem to have the will to live. It was touch and go all the time you were unconscious and Mr Saker was worried out of his mind. You might even say he saved your life, so I think he's at least earned your thanks.'

Thanks! If the nurse only knew! But it was too late to raise any more objections because Benet was already there, freshly shaved but still haggard, and Kirsten could no longer hold her bitter thoughts at bay.

'They tell me you saved my life, though I can't think why.'

'Because I couldn't bear to have your death on my conscience as well as everything else,' he said in a low voice, but he had turned away from her to move the chair nearer the bed and she couldn't see his expression.

She frowned in puzzlement. Did he have a conscience after all, then? She hadn't seen any evidence of it before. And what did he mean, 'As well as everything else?' Then, with a shaft of pain she knew the answer.

'You mean the baby.' She closed her eyes but the tears of desolation squeezed between the lids. 'I suppose I've lost the baby, too.'

There was a lengthy silence and then he said gently, 'Kirsten, there *was* no baby. Of course, I told the doctor when you were brought in here that there was a danger of a miscarriage, but he told me later he'd found no evidence that you'd ever been pregnant.'

'You're lying!' Hysteria welled up like a scalding spring. 'You won't believe *anything* you don't want to believe, will you?' she accused him wildly. 'I never expected you to admit responsibility for it, but to deny it ever existed . . . Next you'll be denying you ever made love to me at all! Or is this just another turn of the screw to punish me?'

He stared at her wordlessly, his face as white as paper, then he turned and walked out of the room.

Kirsten fought back the hysteria. If she'd hurt him, she was glad. Hadn't he taken a vicious enjoyment in hurting her? And wasn't he still trying to hurt her, lying like that?

The door opened again and for a moment Kirsten thought it was Benet returning to the attack, but it was only the doctor. He looked at her chart, felt her pulse and shone a light in her eyes. Then he sat in the chair Benet had so recently vacated.

'Kirsten, may I ask you what led you to believe you were pregnant?'

Kirsten stared at him, the hysteria still not far away. 'Why does any girl have reason to believe it? I hadn't had a period since—since—' Her voice choked, but after a few moments she was able to go on, 'And then there were the fainting attacks and the awful sickness.'

'But you didn't have a pregnancy test?' he pressed. 'You didn't see a doctor and have him confirm it?'

Kirsten was forced to admit she hadn't. 'I didn't feel it needed confirming, it was real enough. Are you trying to tell me Benet was speaking the truth, that I never was pregnant, that I imagined it all?'

'I'm quite certain you didn't imagine anything,' the doctor said soothingly and she suspected him of trying to humour her until he went on, 'In a psychosomatic condition the mind can produce symptoms that are very real to the sufferer.'

'You're trying to say I subconsciously *wanted* to be pregnant? But why in the world would I do that?' she demanded wildly. 'God knows, I already had enough problems.'

The doctor hesitated. 'Mr Saker *did* tell me a little about your circumstances—your engagement and your subsequent estrangement—but I can still only guess. Either the pregnancy was something you desperately wanted or it could have been that subconsciously you were punishing yourself for what you considered a lapse. The only thing I *can* be sure of is that you were not miscarrying when you were brought in here and you are not pregnant now.'

After he had left her, Kirsten lay staring up at the ceiling for a long time. At first she found it impossible to accept what the doctor had said, but as his words kept repeating themselves over and over in her head she began to face the fact that he had told her the truth and that she had never conceived Benet's child. The reasons why her mind had produced such utterly convincing symptoms of pregnancy were even harder to accept, but accept them she did in time.

Although she had been shocked at the idea of having an illegitimate child when the father no longer had any time for her, she had to admit she had desperately wanted the baby, wanted that part of Benet to remind her he *had* loved her once. And she had to admit she could have been punishing herself, too. She had been bitterly hurt when Benet refused to believe she hadn't been a willing partner in Jude's scheme to defraud him and ruin his reputation as an antique art dealer, but looking back on the whole sorry business could she really blame Benet for believing her part in it had been deliberate?

She *should* have been more questioning, less gullible when Jude had first drawn her into his web of deceit. Jude was a trained artist, and a knowledgeable one. Had those drawings of his really been genuine he would have known their value, so would he really have put them into the hands of a two-bit dealer like herself to sell for him, an inexperienced girl he had scraped a casual acquaintance with only a few weeks before? Shouldn't she have suspected his motives when she knew the most reputable dealers in the land would have jumped at the chance to handle the deal?

But she had been too pleased with herself, too ambitious to pull off something big to question seriously anything he'd told her. She had never even considered that being a clever artist he *could* have forged the drawings.

No, even though she hadn't deliberately set out to trick Benet as Jude had made it appear, she must bear some of the blame that the attempt had ever been made at all.

Her conscience began to prick, too, as she remembered the bitter accusations she had flung at Benet. The nurse had told her that if it hadn't been for him sitting by her bed hour after hour willing her to live, she might easily have died, so whatever his motive for coming back into her life, she couldn't go on believing it was for the sick enjoyment of hurting her. It had probably been conscience about the baby. Did that mean then that he would have acknowledged the child as his? That he no longer believed Jude had been her lover and so could just as easily have been the father?

Kirsten moved restlessly on the bed. It was an academic question anyway. There *was* no baby, so if Benet had felt any sense of responsibility, he was relieved of it now. It was unlikely she would ever know the truth of how or why he had sought her out again. Remembering the look on his face when he had last walked out of here, she didn't think he would be back.

She was wrong. The drips had been removed and although she had only managed a bowl of soup for her lunch and a little bread and butter with her cup of tea, she had had a good supper and was leaning back against the pillows when a voice said to the nurse who was collecting her tray, 'Is it all right if I come in?'

'Of course, Mr Saker.' The nurse flashed him a pink-cheeked smile.

Benet closed the door after her but remained there

leaning against it, his eyes wary as if unsure of his welcome, and Kirsten's heart began to thump. 'Did the doctor talk to you?' he asked.

She nodded. 'I'm sorry I wouldn't believe you, but I really did think—' She sighed and went on in a strained voice, 'I can understand your being angry. You must have thought I was trying to trap you into marriage or get money out of you or something.'

'Trap me? When you disappeared without trace?' He crossed the room and sat on the edge of the bed, taking her good hand in his. 'Kirsten, why didn't you tell me you thought you were pregnant?' There was a note in his voice that shivered along her nerve ends and the warmth of his clasp seemed to radiate heat throughout her entire body.

But she couldn't bring herself to look at him as she said huskily, 'I—I tried to once, that day when Mrs Pattinson asked if I could speak to you. But you were making love to Susan. And anyway, what was the point when you still believed Jude and I were lovers? You'd only have said the baby was his.'

Benet groaned as if he was in pain. 'I remember. Oh God, why was I such a stiff-necked fool! Kirsten, long before then, seeing the way you were with your aunt, never thinking about yourself, I knew I must have been wrong about you, but I was too proud to climb down, too sure that I'd already made you hate me anyway, after the way I'd treated you.'

Kirsten let out a long sigh. 'I'm glad if you can really believe I wasn't a deliberate party to Jude's plot, but I still deserved your contempt. If I hadn't been so stupidly gullible as to fall for Jude's story he'd never have been able to use me against you.'

'You weren't to know how devious Jude can be—I did,' he replied in a low voice. 'It wasn't just the forgery plot. It went a whole lot deeper than that. Once Jude knew I was in love with you, it put a real weapon into his hands and he knew it. That's why he wouldn't admit you weren't in the plot, why he tried to give the impression you were already lovers. Kirsten, in my heart of hearts I knew all the time you couldn't have been.'

She trembled, heat diffusing her whole body as he went on, 'I'd already had you, remember? I knew I was the first. But it was like history repeating itself. Jude's father had stolen my mother and now Jude was taking you, the only girl I'd ever loved. I was so maddened by jealousy I couldn't reason any more, I could only lash out and hurt you back.'

Kirsten shut her eyes. She could see now how devastatingly hurtful her apparent deceit must have been for him. That icy contempt, those callous taunts had been a form of self-defence. If he hadn't loved her he couldn't have been hurt so badly. But she noticed he spoke of that love in the past tense and her heart twisted inside her.

'And then your aunt died—' Benet's voice broke and she saw him swallow convulsively. 'All along, Kirsten, you'd denied there was anything between you and Jude, and just when I was about convinced, you admitted you were going to him.' His breathing was ragged. 'Why did you tell me that if it wasn't true?'

Kirsten shook her head helplessly. If only she hadn't! Perhaps then she might have been able to win back his love before it was too late. 'Because you'd never believed me when I denied it before so I couldn't see you believing it then. And it seemed to be what you wanted to hear.'

'Wanted!' His grip on her hand tightened so fiercely that she winced. 'When Susan told me that morning she'd just caught you in the bathroom being sick and you'd admitted you were pregnant, I was *glad*! I thought now I had a lever to keep you away from Jude. But then when I went to look for you, you'd disappeared.' The anguish in his voice echoed the anguish he must have felt.

'I went straight round to his studio, but of course you

weren't there, and when he tried to make out you'd been living with him ever since you came back from Bermuda, I knew he was lying, and I knew with absolute certainty that he'd lied about everything else.' He put his other hand up to her cheek, cupping it against his palm. 'Kirsten, can you ever forgive me? I knew how you'd fought against falling in love with me, and then when I'd forced your surrender, to throw your love back in your face like that . . .'

He sounded as if he really cared, she thought wonderingly. But then remorse wasn't the same as loving, was it. 'Of course I forgive you,' she said softly, carefully keeping her face lowered in case she betrayed her feelings. If he knew how desperately she still loved him he might offer to marry her out of pity and she knew she couldn't bear that.

'I was so relieved you hadn't gone to Jude,' he went on, letting his hand fell away from her face, 'that at first I wasn't too worried. I knew you'd have to keep in touch with the solicitor so I went to see him. Branscombe wasn't at all forthcoming until I told him you were pregnant and that I was responsible, and that I wanted to find you and put things right between us if I could. It was then he told me how little there was going to be for you out of your aunt's estate, and he said you'd known that all along.'

Kirsten nodded. 'You always wondered at the reason for my aunt's matchmaking. That was it.'

Benet groaned again. 'You can imagine how I felt, remembering how I'd jibed at you about your inheritance! I made Branscombe promise to let me know when he heard from you, and a couple of days later he rang me to give me the address of the hotel you were staying in. I missed you by about three hours.

'That was when I really began to get frantic. I rang Branscombe every day, but even when we started putting notices in the national newspapers there was still nothing. God, I never want to go through a time like that again. I couldn't work, I couldn't eat or sleep for thinking of all the terrible things that could have happened to you, alone and pregnant and virtually penniless. And it was all my fault. I'd almost convinced myself you must be dead when I actually *saw* you outside the gallery one day. You just stood there looking, like some frail little ghost, and before I could move you were walking away. I ran after you, calling, but I lost you again in the crowds.'

'You called me?' Her eyes widened. 'And I thought it was only my imagination.' All the time she had been longing for him, believing he had forgotten her existence, he had been trying to find her, wanting to see her, too.

He released her hand and stood up, pacing to the window. 'I cursed myself for not moving faster. But at least I knew you were still alive! I wanted to tear London apart with my bare hands to find you, and all I could do was call in a detective agency and ask them to pull out all the stops, and even that seemed a frail hope when there was nothing to go on. And then Branscombe phoned to say you'd been in touch at last.'

He came back to the bed and stood looking down at her, his eyes haunted. 'Waiting outside your room for you to come back, I thought all my troubles were over—but they were really beginning again worse than ever. Kirsten, why did you run away from me like that? Have I made you hate me so much?'

She longed to reach out her arms to comfort him but she was still too unsure of him to give herself away. 'I never hated you,' she said huskily. 'It—it was such a shock, seeing you standing there, and you seemed so angry.' She licked her dry lips. 'Benet, if you'd really been trying so hard to find me, why were you so angry?'

He dropped to his knees and pulled her into his arms, burying his face against her breast. 'God knows! Why does a parent shout at a child who's been lost? I *know* I was saying all the wrong things, but I couldn't seem to help myself. And then when you fell downstairs and I saw you in a crumpled heap at the bottom . . .' He shuddered violently and her arms tightened around him. 'I shall have nightmares about that for as long as I live.'

He looked up into her face. 'Darling, you said yesterday the nurse had told you I saved your life and you asked me why I bothered. I knew if I let you die, I wouldn't want to go on living either. So I sat there hour after hour, just willing you to come back to me.'

'I know,' she said softly. 'I wanted so much just to float off to where nothing could touch me any more, but you were too strong for me. You kept dragging me back. I know I didn't appear grateful at the time, but I'm glad now.' She reached up and touched the thick dark hair that overnight seemed to have a sprinkling of grey. 'You mustn't go on torturing yourself, Benet.'

He caught her hand and brought it to his mouth. 'Kirsten, I know I've destroyed any love you had for me,' he whispered against her palm, 'but let me make amends. Say you'll marry me and let me look after you.'

Kirsten felt weak with wanting him, desperately tempted to say yes. It was less than the love he had first offered her, but it would be better than nothing, and he obviously needed to salve his conscience. 'Benet, I don't know if marrying me out of pity would work,' she said doubtfully.

'Pity!' His voice cracked in disbelief. 'Dear God, girl, haven't I been telling you how much I need you? How desperately I love you? I never want to let you out of my sight again, ever. I'd even like to think I could teach you to trust me again, even to love me just a little.'

'Just a little!' For a moment her heart was too full to speak and then she laughed shakily. 'Oh catch me, Benet, before I float away!' The look on his face at the reminder of that magic moment in Bermuda brought tears to her eyes, but they were tears of happiness. 'Oh Benet, I never stopped loving you. Oh, I told myself sometimes I hated you, but I never was a good liar.'

'You can be generous enough to say that . . . after all I've done to you?' Kirsten had never heard him speak with such humility, and yet rather than diminishing him it only increased his stature in her eyes.

'After all *Jude's* done,' she reminded him softly, then she clung to him as if to assure herself he really was there in her arms. 'He nearly destroyed us both, Benet, and yet I can only feel sorry for him. Because he didn't succeed, did he? You're here and I'm here, and yes, my darling, of course I'll marry you.'

The joy that blazed in his face was almost worth the past heartbreak. 'Oh, my precious love.' He rocked her in his arms, kissing her mouth, her eyes, her breasts. 'I can't wait to get you out of here. Just as soon as they'll let you you're coming back to my apartment to convalesce. I'll ask Susan to come and look after you until you're well enough for us to get married.'

'Susan!'

He smothered her disconcerted exclamation with another kiss. 'Never even think it, my darling. I'm afraid I' used her badly too, trying to make you jealous. When she realised how things really were between us she was terribly upset about her part in it, and almost as worried as I was over your disappearance. She'd like to set the record straight with you, if you'd let her.'

'Of course I'll let her.' Kirsten smiled, so happy she wanted the whole world to share it. 'I couldn't help liking her even though I was jealous of her,' she admitted.

'I'll tell you now, I won't give you cause to be jealous again, ever,' he promised, the brilliant blue of his eyes softening to an infinite tenderness as he captured her tremulous mouth with his own.

'How do you fancy a honeymoon in Bermuda?' he said softly, releasing her mouth only to transfer his attentions to the lobe of her ear. 'Oh, not at Everleigh. I know my father's longing to see you again, but I don't want to share you even with him, yet. I thought one of those beach cottages on Mangrove Bay.'

'Back to where it all began.' Kirsten sighed blissfully. 'Oh yes, please, Benet. I *would* enjoy that.'

He held her head between his hands, looking down into her face, his eyes lingering lovingly over every feature. 'And I'm going to enjoy spending the rest of my life looking after you and showing you just how much you mean to me, darling,' he said quietly.